'Hello, Alex.' Daniel's voice, unchanged and deeply moving, made her shiver.

'Hello, Daniel.'

'It's been a long time,' he replied.

Not long enough, a voice rasped inside her head as memories mentally tagged 'irretrievable' came tumbling back. Daniel beside her, the young Daniel, his dark hair flicking playfully over the collar of his shirt. The carpet of leaves on which they lay, her first and unquestionable experience of sex as he drew her safely and magically into womanhood.

Alex blinked, and returned to the present with a sickening thud.

'Alex—are you okay?' Daniel put his arm around her, the strong grip that had suffered no change over the years sliding firmly around her waist. in uproar at his to

GW00702279

Carol Wood lives with her artist husband on the south coast of England. She has always taken an interest in medical matters, especially general practice and nursing in the community. Her hobbies are walking by the sea, watching wildlife and, of course, reading and writing romantic fiction.

Recent titles by the same author:

HER PARTNER'S PASSION
BACK IN HER BED
THE PATIENT DOCTOR*
THE HONOURABLE DOCTOR*

Country Partners duo

THE IRRESISTIBLE DOCTOR

BY
CAROL WOOD

To Phyllis
Happy hours
with my book.
Carol
x

MILLS & BOON®

DID YOU PURCHASE THIS BOOK WITHOUT A COVER?

If you did, you should be aware it is **stolen property** as it was reported *unsold and destroyed* by a retailer. Neither the author nor the publisher has received any payment for this book.

All the characters in this book have no existence outside the imagination of the author, and have no relation whatsoever to anyone bearing the same name or names. They are not even distantly inspired by any individual known or unknown to the author, and all the incidents are pure invention.

All Rights Reserved including the right of reproduction in whole or in part in any form. This edition is published by arrangement with Harlequin Enterprises II B.V. The text of this publication or any part thereof may not be reproduced or transmitted in any form or by any means, electronic or mechanical, including photocopying, recording, storage in an information retrieval system, or otherwise, without the written permission of the publisher.

This book is sold subject to the condition that it shall not, by way of trade or otherwise, be lent, resold, hired out or otherwise circulated without the prior consent of the publisher in any form of binding or cover other than that in which it is published and without a similar condition including this condition being imposed on the subsequent purchaser.

MILLS & BOON and MILLS & BOON with the Rose Device are registered trademarks of the publisher.

First published in Great Britain 2002
Harlequin Mills & Boon Limited,
Eton House, 18-24 Paradise Road, Richmond, Surrey TW9 1SR

© Carol Wood 2002

ISBN 0 263 83102 7

Set in Times Roman 10¼ on 11¼ pt.
03-1102-52823

Printed and bound in Spain
by Litografía Rosés, S.A., Barcelona

CHAPTER ONE

PERHAPS because she was still thinking of Ollie's tear-filled eyes and wishing there was something she could do to help, Dr Alexandra Trent walked into her colleague's room without knocking.

At just gone eight on a post-August Bank Holiday morning, she had expected to find Peter sitting comfortably in his chair with an overflowing mug of coffee balanced indecently close to the edge of his desk and a pair of thoughtful hazel eyes trained on the ceiling above.

Peter's professional but utterly relaxed concentration was only engaged after an earnest liquid meditation. And since the Bank Holiday Monday had probably been busier for Peter, who had been on call throughout, there seemed every reason to expect to find him enjoying an especially unhurried morning ritual.

Fleetingly, as her hand pushed against the door, she thought she heard voices coming from inside. But, since Tyllington Surgery staff were busily preparing for the day ahead, she had no reason to detect the soft murmurs.

Nor, stupidly, did she at first recognise the broad-backed figure sitting in the patient's chair. Inclined forward, even the shape of the muscular male shoulders strained against the white cotton of his shirt gave her no indication as to who Peter's early visitor was.

But it was when her gaze flickered down to the deeply tanned forearms that the memories began to filter through. Slow at first, like tiny drops of rain pattering on glass. And then the full storm as her eyes tumbled down to the solid gold watch. There, amongst the forest of black hair, the familiar square shape was strapped to his wrist and her heart crashed against her ribs. The watch she had given him for his twenty-sixth birthday nine years before.

Slowly he turned, and clear grey eyes sparkled and glinted under swirls of silver as his gaze focused and locked with hers.

Unconscious though it was, her senses leapt to the only conclusion. The assumption that she had been caught up in some kind of time warp and at any moment the picture would fizzle and fade and her sanity return.

Then *wham*. Her body's more realistic reaction to shock: air sucked into her lungs as if she'd been slammed hard against a wall by an invisible hand, the top of her head spinning into the ether like a shooting star.

'Alex, wonderful—you're in early!' Dr Peter Barlow laughed softly, delight and enthusiasm in his eyes. 'Couldn't wait for you to arrive. Look who's here. It's Daniel—Daniel Hayward—remember?'

Oh, yes. She remembered.

She remembered very well.

The tall figure rose, unravelling his long, lean frame inch by inch. The change in his appearance was as disturbing as it was mesmerising and Alex stared incredulously at the man she had last seen nine years ago. Compared to the rugby-playing student of those times this man was gaunt and spare, with honed cheeks that cracked upward as he made an effort to smile.

'Hello, Alex.' His voice, unchanged and deeply moving, made her shiver. Dragging back her shoulders, she nodded.

'Hello, Daniel.'

'It's been a long time.'

Not long enough, a voice rasped inside her head as memories mentally tagged 'Irretrievable' came tumbling back. Daniel beside her, the young Daniel, his dark hair flicking playfully over the collar of his rugby shirt. The carpet of leaves on which they lay. Her first and unquestionable experience of sex as he drew her safely and magically into womanhood. The end-of-year student party in the hospital annexe, his body pressed against hers as they moved as one on the dance floor. Heat from his broad chest and flat abdomen shamelessly burning her, claiming her slight, fragile body as his own.

Alex blinked, and returned to the present with a sickening thud. Her blonde lashes flickered as her hand moved upward to push shakily at the curtain of natural blonde hair that fell across her face.

'Alex—are you okay?' her colleague asked in concern. But it was Daniel who moved forward, as light on his long legs as he had ever been, crossing the floor and reaching out.

His arm went around her—a strong grip that had suffered no change over the years—sliding firmly around her waist and guiding her to the chair. She sank down, her senses in uproar at his touch.

'I'm fine—thank you.' She shrank away from him, ashamed of her reaction. 'I'm okay now. Really.'

'You don't look too bright,' Peter objected, peering at her.

'I'm fine,' she argued again, then conceded, 'I rushed this morning...skipped breakfast.' A concession she would never make normally. But it was worth it today and seemed to satisfy Peter.

'Look—I'll come back later...' Daniel said beside her. She dragged her reluctant gaze up and prayed for strength. She took in everything then. Had to force herself, of course, but she couldn't let him see—or Peter see—that she was shattered. Somehow she had to hang on.

Daniel Hayward had indeed changed, she found herself thinking as she took in every last detail, unable to stop the hungry passage of her eyes. So tall and lean now, eyes almost haunted, hair cropped to reveal a strong, unbelievably handsome skull that looked more fitting for an ancient warrior. Shoulders that were honed so sparingly yet, oddly, looked strong enough to support the world.

But nothing she could identify could account for the kind

of presence that had her heart pounding, as though she were scenting him like a wild animal, nose to the wind.

Instinct, past and present memory and hunger tussled wildly inside her. A physical hunger that she remembered only too vividly. Even their studies had come a poor second to their shameful desire. Both of them had known it was obsession. And neither of them had been able to fight it.

And even now, as she met those bottomless eyes, shadowed by a darkness that caused his deep sunburn to pale, she felt the irresistible pull to be with him. Her small, seemingly delicate frame, though much stronger than anyone might suspect at first glance, trembled. Her limbs ached for him. And somewhere down low inside her a heat flowed and swirled, making her ashamed once more.

Alex swallowed, dragged her eyes back to Peter and prayed for time.

'I'll get Ollie to make coffee,' Peter said, and reached for the phone, but Alex shook her head.

'No, Peter, not Ollie. She's not well. She's—' Alex stopped and cleared her throat, unable to share Ollie's sad news just yet. 'I had a coffee at home, thanks anyway.'

Peter paused in concern, then shrugged. 'If you're sure?'

'Absolutely.' She swallowed carefully and turned. 'So...Daniel. What brings you to the New Forest?'

Cautious grey eyes met hers. They flickered, burned, then settled like fire on water. 'I knew Peter was in Tyllington,' he told her quietly. 'I had a few days to myself and thought I would—'

'Look an old friend up,' Peter finished enthusiastically. 'But just on the week you were on leave, Alex.'

Daniel's brow twisted. 'On leave? Then you work here, Alex?'

'Lord, I forgot to say,' Peter burst out before Alex could reply. 'Alex has been with us for the last six months as our locum. I don't know what Sean and I would have done without her. Can't begin to think what we'll do when she goes back.'

'To where?' Daniel asked.

'St Mary's General, Portsmouth,' Alex said, adding hesitantly, 'A&E.'

'But…' Daniel began, and then frowned again, 'I thought you were going for surgery…'

'That was a long time ago,' she murmured, and lowered her eyes. 'It never worked out.'

They'd both wanted so much in those days, before that summer of madness. Her ambition hadn't faltered until Daniel. Then nothing had seemed to count. As though someone had cast a spell and all that had mattered was being with him. It had been the same for him too. For a while anyway, until that last terrible row…

It was Peter who broke the awkward silence. 'Of course—you don't know about Alex's accident, Dan. How stupid of me. How long ago was it, Alex?'

'Almost a year.'

'The poor girl injured her back,' Peter continued without drawing a breath. 'On a wretched ski slope, of all things. It was bed-rest for a bit, then, as luck would have it, she signed on with us as a temporary resident. I saw my chance and suggested she come in and try a couple of hours. Smooth her path back to the rigours of Casualty—or a partnership with us, if I could persuade her.' He sighed deeply. 'But unfortunately this lady's heart is already spoken for.'

Alex was aware of Daniel stiffening. Then he did something so impossibly familiar that she fought not to shiver at the sight of it. She recalled the gesture so well. The thrust of the handsome square jaw with its ebony shadow that never seemed quite shaven. The white teeth trapping a lip. A moment's concentrated thought and then the sensual full mouth spreading into a smile that wreaked havoc inside her.

'And—are you better?' His voice was low, concerned.

She nodded. 'I'm getting there.'

Peter shifted in his chair. 'Daniel's been working abroad, Alex.'

Daniel nodded and added quietly, 'Delhi.'

Delhi. Of course. She should have guessed; somewhere incredibly hot and most likely Third World. The deep, deep tan and the hollowed cheeks, the long sinewy body and taut abdomen that showed through his shirt...

'I work with the World Health Organisation,' he explained, mirroring her thoughts. 'Last year I was Delhi-based—a children's charity.' He sighed briefly and raised his palms. 'Look, I won't keep you. I can see you have a busy morning ahead.' He ran a hand through hair as thick and dark as ever. But the untidy student style had been replaced by the short, economical crop of the traveller. 'Peter—I'm not certain that we should expand on...er...last week's idea,' he added hesitantly. 'I'd rather we sat on it for a bit. Think things over.'

At this Peter looked horrified. 'My dear man—it's all arranged! What is there to expand on? When Alex goes we'll be horribly depleted. There's no question we need you.'

'You mean,' Alex blurted, 'you've offered Daniel a position here?'

Peter looked puzzled. 'Well, yes, that's the general idea. We've been looking for some time, as you know, but Daniel said he can stay here temporarily until he goes back to...'

'Nothing has been decided,' Daniel cut in swiftly. 'I've no intention of upsetting you, Alex. It was just an idea.'

Peter came round the desk and gently laid his hand on Alex's shoulder. His forehead was furrowed and his hazel eyes shadowed. 'Alex, this isn't like you. You're not feeling so good this morning, are you? It's your back, isn't it?'

'Maybe I overdid it a little last week,' she faltered.

'I knew it!' Peter exclaimed. 'You should have rested on your week off.'

'It's nothing,' Alex insisted. 'I'm...I'm happy you've found someone.'

'That's my girl.' Peter smiled. 'I knew you'd be delighted…' He tailed off, still a little uncertain of her reaction. 'And, anyway, if you *both* decide to stay four partners isn't out of the question. In fact, it would be terrific.'

Alex pulled herself together. She mustn't let either Peter or Daniel see how shaken she was. Although from the way both of them were staring at her, it seemed she'd revealed far too much already.

'Tempting, Peter,' she said, and smiled brightly. 'But general practice isn't my field. Though I have to admit the last six months have been wonderful. If it hadn't been for you I would have gone back to A&E too early and probably burned myself out.' She got up shakily. 'Having said that, I have a surgery to take.'

'Are you sure you're up to it this morning?' Peter enquired doubtfully.

'No problem,' she assured him, and turned. But as she reached the door Daniel was there before her.

'Alex, I'm really sorry…'

'For what?' she answered tightly.

'I had no idea you were working here.'

She gazed into the glimmering pools of liquid mercury that held her soft blue eyes. 'It makes no difference to me whether you did or didn't, Daniel. I'm not a partner here. I've no say in the matter. And, to be honest, I won't be around long enough to care.'

Somehow—she wasn't quite sure how—she got to her room and trawled through morning surgery. It was close to the beginning of the autumn term and there were coughs and colds and abundant pre-school irritations. But they were only minor ailments, and the flow of feet ceased around midday.

Her disciplined order of mind soon crumbled as she remembered Daniel. Was he still here somewhere under the practice roof? Had he accepted Peter's offer? Alex closed her eyes and sifted through her scattered thoughts. Like sheep, she had to usher them back into order, priorities first. And then she remembered Ollie—the receptionist.

'How is Ollie?' she asked, ringing through to Pauline Harris at Reception. Alex was aware that most of the staff had witnessed Ollie's breakdown early this morning, and it was Pauline who had comforted her in the office.

'She's gone home, Dr Trent. I just can't believe it. She and Grant have been married for twenty years. They were the happiest couple I knew.'

'Yes, it's very sad,' Alex sighed, unable to imagine Ollie's pain at being faced with a young woman arriving at the house that morning, claiming she was having an affair with Ollie's husband. 'Pauline, is Ollie on her own? I wondered if I should call after surgery.'

'She's got a sister living in Tyllington. Dr Hayward phoned her and told her what had happened. She was going to Ollie's straight away.'

Alex took a breath. 'Dr Hayward? How did he know? Has he spoken to Ollie?'

'Yes, he talked to her for quite a while. Up in the staff-room. Made her a cup of tea and then took her home. Oh, he's just arriving back. Do you want to talk to him?'

'No,' Alex said quickly. 'I'll catch up with him later, Pauline.' But seconds later there was a knock on the door and she heard Daniel's voice as he opened it slowly.

Just watching him move made her heart beat faster. Un-hurried and casual, he seemed to have no concerns about violating her space. Which he was. He might not think about it in that way, but even the air he breathed seemed in some way linked to her.

'Have you time to stop?' he asked as he came across the room. 'Do you take a lunch hour?'

She shuffled the patient records on her desk and kept her eyes lowered. 'Not today, Daniel. I've too much to do.'

'I'd like to talk to you, Alex. It's important.'

She lowered her head and sank back against the chair. 'Daniel, why did you come here? Why this part of the world? You had the whole planet to choose from.'

He moved forward. 'That's why I need to talk to you—to explain.'

'No, Daniel—'

'Alex, please. We must. You know that.'

'No,' she argued. 'There's no reason for us to talk. Not if you don't take up Peter's offer.'

His eyes tangled with hers. 'You'd prefer it if I refused the job?'

A wave of anger rippled through her. Why did he think she would agree? What gave him the right to walk back into her life after all these years and expect her to welcome him?

'I know what you're thinking, Alex,' he went on huskily. 'And I swear I don't want to upset you. Just give me half an hour. That's all I ask. No more. And if you still want me to go, I will. You have my word.'

She sucked in air. 'What have you told Peter?'

'Nothing—yet.'

'He doesn't know about you and I,' she said flatly. 'Just that we knew one another.'

'In which case we could keep it that way.' He shrugged easily.

'I couldn't do it, Daniel,' she told him honestly, and looked up. 'It would seem somehow dishonest not to explain.'

'All the more reason why we should talk, then,' he countered. 'And settle unfinished business.'

'It was finished the day you walked out of my life,' she said, and felt her heart pound at the memory.

'There were reasons, Alex—'

'Daniel, no,' she protested wearily. 'Not here.'

There were sounds in the corridor and his shoulders rose, then dropped heavily as someone approached. 'All right.' He nodded. 'Where?'

If it hadn't been for the footsteps she might have held out. But they came closer and she said quickly, 'Do you remember Marl Wood?'

He nodded. 'I remember.'

'I'll be there at six.'

He threw her one last look, hesitated briefly, then strode from the room, leaving her wondering what in the world she had done.

Marl Wood.

It was safe there, at least. A quiet little wood that sheltered a bright, quick stream and afforded privacy. Where, years ago, they had walked the dog and strolled hand in hand. And where, on that last day, they had parted. Mixed memories—enough to remind them of just how much a disaster their affair had been.

As Alex finished her day she decided to discover if Sean Ashley, Peter's partner, had met Daniel yet. It was with faint hope that she caught up with him as they left.

The little town was busy with tourists. Tyllington Surgery nestled at the heart of it all, the green-tiled roof and white walls a picture-postcard setting amongst the shops. Alex always wondered how Peter had had the vision to build the surgery there six years ago. Many would have withered at the initial opposition. The previous health centre had caused problems with the traffic and been moved to the outskirts.

But Peter's quiet determination had resulted in talking everyone round. The council had made a one-way route and the residents had agreed. In no time at all Peter's unobtrusive practice building had been in place.

Their list had grown steadily. Sean had joined almost immediately, and then a female doctor. She'd now left, to raise a family, and since Alex's accident Peter had persuaded her into 'a couple of quiet days locuming'.

But it had proved anything but quiet. Challenging, demanding and wonderfully satisfying, but never quiet. Two days had become three, then four as her health improved. And now, as she strolled beside the tall figure of Sean after yet another hectic day, Alex had to admit that she had been her happiest here.

And that was the way she wanted things to stay. At least until she left. Then Daniel Hayward could do what he liked. If it came to it, Alex thought as she talked to Sean, perhaps she could even leave before Christmas. Hadn't she always planned to pick up the threads at A&E?

'How do you feel about Daniel Hayward?' Alex asked bravely as she accompanied Sean across the car park after surgery.

'Very positive,' Sean said, to her niggling disappointment. 'He's a nice guy. I think we'll get on rather well. You know each other, I gather?'

She nodded. 'Yes, in London, nine years ago. I was in my second year; Daniel was coming up to his Finals.'

'So it must have been quite a surprise seeing him again? Or had you kept in contact?'

'No, we hadn't,' she answered swiftly. 'You know how it is.'

'Indeed I do. One always means to write, or even to phone, but one gets caught up in other things.'

'Yes,' she agreed, and decided that she stood no chance of meeting anyone who didn't like Daniel—but then, who wouldn't? He was a great guy—just so long as you didn't fall in love with him, she thought bitterly.

They reached their cars and Sean perched on the bonnet of his, a neat green sports with a cream soft top. 'How about you, Alex?' he asked, brushing back his fair hair, a curious smile breaking across his face. 'You seem to like it here. Can't we persuade you to stay?'

'I'm a hopeless A&E case.' She smiled. 'I'd miss the adrenalin.'

'Well, if it's adrenalin you want—' he grinned '—no doubt we could crank up a bit more for you here. You're part of the furniture now.'

'Thanks,' she chuckled. 'Which part?'

They both laughed and Alex decided to leave it at that. She said goodnight to Sean and got into her car, resigning herself to the fact that if she harboured any reservations about Daniel working at the surgery it was she alone who had them.

It was five-thirty when she drove out of the car park and through the one-way system towards the wood. Alex had considered going home to change from her light summer dress and sandals into something fresh. But her mother's house was fifteen minutes away and both her mother and Cosmo would want to know where she was going. A seven-year-old son's curiosity and her mother's concern would take far longer than a few minutes to satisfy.

So she headed through the New Forest towards Marl, relieved the evening traffic was thinning. Supper wasn't until seven and they never expected her home before six. To her surprise Daniel was there, slightly early as she was.

The sight of a dark blue saloon car and Daniel's tall figure leaning against it gave her a knee-jerk reaction of alarm. But as she negotiated the first cattle grid and drove into the clearing of trees she composed herself, at least enough to park beside him and ignore the crazy flicker of her pulse.

Her hand slipped slightly on the wheel and she came to a jerky halt, but even this she was able to deal with. She actually managed a smile through the window and climbed out, telling herself she was okay—she was fine.

And she was. Until he walked towards her. And then she went to pieces. Quirky kicks of her heart, her pulse beating so loudly she could hear it—and her legs totally gone at the knees.

Daniel had changed. Thigh-hugging jeans and a black T-shirt emphasised his tan. One hand was crammed into a pocket, the outline of narrow hips accentuating the long plane of his legs. Sneakers looked snug, as though he'd been ready all his life for an adventure. She wondered how many countries he travelled to and how many oceans he'd crossed.

His eyes held the heavy expression that made her think of a man who had been pushing himself. Trying to catch his tail, as her mother would have said. And maybe she was right. Was Daniel Hayward still looking? she wondered. For the ultimate career? The greatest challenge? Or were they shadows that mirrored sleepless nights and work-filled days?

'I'm glad you came,' he said quietly as his eyes unself-consciously feasted on her.

Reluctant to hold his gaze, she smoothed the soft folds of her summer dress over her warm thighs and pretended almost not to hear. Instead she glanced across the common laced with summer trees and dense undergrowth. A few metres on and the stream would be echoing over little pebbles that moved to and fro beneath the gentle current.

'Let's take the path,' she murmured, and they walked in silence towards the narrow ribbon of shingle under the trees. Marl was beautiful in summer. Hot and crusty and simmering, even in the glades. But in autumn it would be paradise. A carpet of golden leaves, mulching across woodland. Pigs foraging for acorns in the oak woods and the ponies left to please themselves after the busiest season.

But now it was late August and the summer was clinging on to its last. Her body felt hot under her dress and her nape-length bob felt better pushed away from her face, behind her ears. Out of habit, she turned a glossy wing behind her ear, and suddenly felt his eyes on her. Daniel had stopped and was watching her.

'Don't run away from me, Alex. I won't hurt you.' He was standing in the shadow of the trees, his dark face crumpled in an expression of dismay.

'I won't allow you to,' she said, and faced him.

'I suppose I asked for that.'

'It happened once. You walked out of my life.'

He moved slowly towards her across the sandy path and into the sunlight that dappled the trees. It was soft and silent in there and his breathing was shallow. 'You gave me an ultimatum, Alex. I didn't want to leave you; you just gave me no choice.'

'What did you want, then? Certainly not us.'

'Of course I wanted us. But we were young then. You were twenty, for heaven's sake, too young.'

'Old enough to fall in love.' She felt her lips dry and she licked them nervously. 'To be willing to sacrifice anything for us.'

His eyes glimmered as he stared at her. 'Which is exactly why we had to cool it, Alex. I had my Finals and you had a long slog ahead of you. We were so tangled up with each other. Obsessed. We would have lost everything if we'd gone on so intensely.'

'We could have made it,' she murmured, hardly audible now, even to herself. 'We could have, if hadn't been—'

'For my family,' he muttered coldly. 'That's it, isn't it? It was them or you, and you made me choose. Here, in Marl, you told me I had to choose. You said we wouldn't make it if I kept going home. But what could I do, Alex? Dad was ill, very ill; they needed me.'

'And I needed you.'

'I know.' He moved forward again and reached out, taking her arms and looking into her eyes. 'I was torn apart. I wanted to be with you more than anything. But I just couldn't ignore them. Would you have wanted me to?'

'You're twisting things,' she protested, unable to think because he was so near, because his hands were on her skin and his touch was driving her crazy. And nothing seemed to matter again, except the way she wanted him, unchanged over the years, her need greater than ever.

'If things are twisted, then it was us who twisted them, Alex. And now we've got a chance to put them right. Nine years is a long time,' he whispered softly, and she felt his breath on her cheek and saw his mouth coming down. There was nothing she could do about it as her heart seemed to turn in her chest and his lips covered her own with a sweetness that brought back every other kiss they had shared in that other lifetime.

CHAPTER TWO

HER lids fluttered down and her hands snaked around him, hesitant at first, then he pulled her against him and she hugged him close. His mouth moved over hers as though it had never forgotten the way they kissed. Passion spilled into her mouth with a white-hot heat as their bodies closed together.

It was a cocktail of all the emotions she had forgotten: the flick of his tongue, the pressure of his mouth, his scent. And the small murmurings, the intake of sharp, gasped breath. Everything exactly as she remembered. Only better. Sweeter. More intoxicating than ever before.

She knew it was the same for him. How she knew she wasn't quite certain. But time had distilled the memories and overlaid the present. His hands locked behind her, against her back and she leaned into him, oblivious of time and place.

His kiss went on with a relentless need that matched her own. His mouth closed again over hers and the touch of his fingertips on her neck, driving into her hair, made her shudder.

Then somewhere in the distance she heard a voice, a young voice, like Cosmo's. Borne on the breeze and through the trees. A sound that brought her back to the present, wrapping around her like a gentle warning. She gulped air and pushed away, her lips throbbing from their kiss.

'Alex,' he groaned, and held her. 'Stay with me…'

But she shook her head and gained a footing, and, drawing her hands over her face, she held them to her eyes for one moment. Then she slowly dropped her fingers and focused determinedly on the shimmering trees. When she had recovered, she walked back to the car and leaned against it in the evening sun.

She breathed again, grateful for reality, that the moment of madness had passed. When she turned he was beside her, watching, those grey pools of shadowed mercury glimmering under black lashes. His hands were pushed down into his pockets, his back against the door of his car. He looked lean and hungry and she wanted him all over again. Her body yearned to satisfy the hunger. But she knew better now.

Glancing across the common, she saw the young family. A man and woman and young boy, walking a dog, enjoying the late-evening sun. It was as if fate was reminding her that she too had responsibilities.

Their laughter echoed and she thought of Cosmo at home. 'I have too much to lose to be reckless, Daniel,' she told him evenly. 'I have a son now. A family. And no room in it for the past.'

'A son?' His voice was shocked.

'His name is Cosmo. He's seven.'

His silence told her that he hadn't known, and, glancing down at her hand, he frowned. 'You don't wear a ring.'

'I've never been married,' she replied, and wondered what the expression was in his eyes. He'd never known about Zak—obviously. She'd wondered if someone might have told him all those years ago. But now she could see he was truly shocked.

'Seven,' he repeated, his frown deepening as he eased himself from the car. 'Two years after—'

'After we split up, yes.'

His eyes glimmered then, with something hard and cold, as he asked, 'Who was it?'

'No one you knew,' she replied quickly. 'A friend of a friend. Zak's involved in theatre. I went to his first night and we were introduced afterwards. We dated for a while, but the offer of work abroad came up. Zak wanted to go...'

'And you didn't tell him about the baby?'

'No, not then. I wrote to him after Cosmo was born.'

He stiffened. 'What happened to your training?'

'It wasn't easy,' she admitted. 'I dropped out, and after Cossie's birth managed to find a crèche. I got back to studying pretty quickly, though my grand plan...' she laughed without humour '...becoming a surgeon...well, that was over. I wanted time to be with Cosmo—he came first.'

The air was still around them, and she could see by his expression that he was shaken. After a while he asked, 'Is—Zak—still part of your life?'

She nodded. 'Most years he flies over from wherever he is and visits. He was here this summer.'

He stared at her, then, when she thought he was about to say something, he gave a small grunt instead and an almost imperceptible shake. 'Well, I'm sorry,' he muttered abruptly. 'I seem to have taken a lot for granted.' His grey eyes tangled with hers. 'I'll go, if that's what you want.'

Her blue eyes wavered. 'Do you need to take this job?'

'No,' he admitted, running his hand slowly over his chin, then thrusting it through his hair. 'But I have to recharge. You see, I rather ran out of energy, and Peter's offer came just at the right time.'

It was then that Alex realised how tired he was. Exhaustion hollowed his cheeks and haunted his eyes and it was this that made her weaken.

'It seems we've both been in the wars a little,' he murmured.

She nodded slowly. 'You could say that.'

With a weary lift of his shoulders he smiled. 'Don't worry. I'll have a word with Peter tomorrow. Explain I've decided against it.'

He gazed at her for a few moments, and once more she had the feeling he was about to say something, but he finally turned, the broad back under the black T-shirt straining as he walked to his car.

His long legs covered the ground that only moments before

they had stood on, closely entwined. He didn't look back, and it was only when she heard the soft purr of the engine that Alex made her decision.

She reached the car as it was about to move off, raising her hands for him to stop. He braked so suddenly that she heard the spin of the wheels on the gravel, and he opened the door and jumped out.

'What's wrong?' he asked as he came towards her.

'I don't have the right,' she said as a shaft of sunlight trapped them, 'to ask you to turn the job down. If there is one thing I can vouch for, it's that the New Forest is the best place on earth to find strength.'

'But you wouldn't be happy, Alex, if I stayed.'

'I'm leaving after Christmas,' she said with a sigh of defeat. 'Perhaps it will work until then. I'm willing to try.'

'Do you mean that?'

'I think so.' Her fair lashes flickered. 'But you do understand—about us?'

'I understand.' His eyes were still shadowed and her heart gave a leap of pity. But his parting words went some way to reassuring her as she drove home that evening, in the opposite direction to the sleek blue car that had headed for the motorway.

'I'll keep out of your way, Alex,' he'd promised. 'You won't even know I'm there.'

Daniel kept to his word.

Other than talking to her about their receptionist, for the next week she barely saw him. Ollie Durrant had taken a few days' leave, which was not surprising in the circumstances. And it had fallen to Daniel to make a follow-up visit after his first one.

'Ollie's staying with her sister,' he told Alex on Friday morning, before surgery started. 'Just until things are sorted out. I said I'd call in over the weekend.'

'Poor Ollie,' Alex sighed.

'Come with me, if you like,' Daniel said quietly. His expression was guarded, and before she could reply he added stiffly, 'I only suggest that because I feel a bit of an interloper. I'm not her official GP and I haven't known her for long.'

'You were there for her when she needed to talk,' Alex replied, aware that she had been, in a sense, a little relieved at not being drawn into Ollie's domestic problems. Daniel was new on the scene and therefore could be more objective.

'Doesn't her little girl, Emma, go to school with your son?'

Alex nodded. 'Tyllington Primary—they're in the same class. But school hasn't started yet so Cossie hasn't seen Emma recently.'

'Would he like to?' Daniel suggested. 'I have the feeling it might help.'

'In what way?'

'A touch of normality wouldn't go amiss. Why don't you give Ollie a ring?'

'I don't know,' Alex replied hesitantly. 'I'll think about it.'

And that was the only conversation they shared. Not that time had allowed for more. The surgery was busy with the last trickle of holiday makers, and Peter had suggested that Daniel hold a clinic for temporary residents and emergencies. Alex had to admit that this had eased things for herself and Sean, and twice during the week she had been home earlier than usual.

'Things are working out with Daniel?' her mother commented that evening as, after dinner, they sat in the conservatory and talked. Alex had anticipated her mother's reaction to Daniel's appearance as being unfazed. Helen Trent had liked the young Daniel Hayward, the handsome young medical student her daughter had brought home. And Alex had never given her reason to feel otherwise.

'Yes, I suppose.' Alex was watching her son through the wide glass windows of the country house. His fair hair flopped untidily over his forehead as he played football in the garden and her mother's sheepdog, Suzie, barked at his heels.

'Is it difficult for you, darling?' Helen asked quietly. 'Being with him again?'

'I was concerned it might be,' Alex admitted as she balanced her bare heels on the edge of the coffee table and plucked at the hem of her shorts. 'But Daniel seems professional. It's up to both of us to be, isn't it? The fact that we went out for one summer years ago shouldn't affect our working relationship now.'

Helen Trent, petite and fair-haired, like her daughter, smiled dryly. 'That's good to hear. And friendship is important.'

Alex glanced at her mother. She wondered what she was really thinking, since she had never confided the true reason for her break-up with Daniel.

'As a matter of fact Daniel suggested a combined visit to Ollie,' Alex said distractedly, the problem of whether she should ring Ollie still at the back of her mind. 'She's staying with her sister June. Emma's there too.'

'Yes, I saw June in Tyllington,' her mother said, and Alex looked across in surprise.

'When?'

'This morning. In the supermarket. June suggested much the same. She feels Ollie is a little isolated. I almost said I'd call in, but I don't know Ollie that well. Only from seeing her in Reception. I did wonder if you were going to visit.'

Alex wasn't really surprised her mother had bumped into June. A widow of ten years, Helen involved herself in the community and knew everyone in Tyllington. Peter was her GP and it was Peter she had suggested Alex consult after her accident. 'Well, I suppose I should,' Alex pondered. 'I'll ring first.'

'Good idea.' Her mother stood up and pulled on a sweater

over her casual cords. 'I'm taking Suzie for a walk, darling. I'll ask Cossie if he wants to come too.'

Alex watched her mother walk through the conservatory doors and into the garden. Her heart gave a little squeeze as Cosmo ran up and took hold of the lead, threading it around Suzie's furry black-and-white neck. He was very close to his grandmother and it showed.

Not for the first time Alex counted her blessings. Her mother remained in good health, even after her father's death. They had been close and he was still missed. But the massive heart attack that had taken him when she was nineteen had been thankfully swift. As a surgeon, he had dreaded the idea of a long and inescapable illness, the prospect of disability. He had led a full and happy life, he'd always said. And both Alex and her mother comforted themselves with this thought.

Alex sighed and wandered to the window. Cossie and his grandmother squeezed through the gate at the bottom of the garden and disappeared into the forest beyond.

She was very lucky. Not only did she have a healthy and active mother who cherished her grandson, but she had a wonderful place in which to recuperate. She had almost completely recovered from her skiing accident. The only shadow in her life was Daniel.

Well, she could handle it…if she was careful. Exert some discipline over mind and body. The months would pass quickly and she would move on, return to A&E and resume her old way of life.

More confidently Alex turned from the window, rooted out the address book and dialled June Masters's number.

She didn't feel quite so confident, though, when she saw Daniel on Sunday afternoon. He was walking towards them, his long legs moving casually down the narrow lane towards June Masters's terraced house. There weren't many people around. A few shops were open, but the vast majority were closed. He was taller than most men and very distinctive, with his short dark crop and deep tan. Her hand momentarily tightened on Cosmo's shoulder.

Thank God she had Cossie. She had to keep things in proportion and Cossie would help her do just that. Seeing Daniel always caught her off guard, his height and understated good looks more unnerving than ever. And out of surgery hours his presence seemed even more daunting.

'Is this Dr Hayward?' Cosmo said, and Alex wondered if it had been sensible of her to explain beforehand that they were meeting an old friend of hers. Cosmo hadn't let the subject drop. He was curious to know who Daniel was.

'Yes, it is,' she answered hesitantly.

A smile broke over Daniel's face as they met on the pavement. He slid one large hand out of his pocket.

'You must be Cosmo,' Daniel said, taking Cosmo's small hand and shaking it gently.

Alex watched her son's blue eyes run curiously over the tall figure dressed casually in light-coloured chinos and a short-sleeved white T-shirt. She waited apprehensively. They made an arresting picture and for a second or two her heart missed a beat.

'You and Emma are friends?' Daniel asked and Cosmo nodded.

'She's not exactly my best friend,' Cosmo said gravely. 'But she's in my class. We do play, but girls are a bit bossy.'

Daniel laughed. 'I'm sure she'll be pleased to see you.'

'Mummy said you've been to India,' Cosmo said, and Alex blushed.

'Yes, I worked there for a while,' Daniel answered, still smiling.

'Did you see any elephants?'

'A few. Why? Do you like elephants?'

'I've never seen a real one. But I watch them on TV.'

'They are quite something,' Daniel agreed, his hand resting lightly on the boy's shoulder. 'And they look much more majestic in the wild.'

'In the wild?' Cosmo repeated, his eyes widening.

'Yes, in Africa. I was there for a while too.'

'My friend Michael went on safari,' Cosmo chattered on. 'And he said that—'

'Cossie,' Alex broke in gently, 'we came to visit Emma. I think we'd better do just that.'

Cosmo grinned, his blue eyes twinkling as he gazed up at Daniel. 'Will you tell me about Africa one day?'

Daniel glanced at Alex. 'Well, maybe. But now I think we'd better say hello to your friend.'

They moved on and Alex breathed a sigh of relief. Cosmo was not normally so talkative and she hadn't anticipated the way he had taken to Daniel. It unsettled her a little.

'So you decided to come,' Daniel said as they walked.

'Yes, I phoned Ollie.'

'I was hoping you would,' he murmured, slanting her a glance. 'I mean, it will make things easier—for Ollie.'

She wasn't quite certain what he meant and even felt that wasn't quite what he'd been going to say, but she didn't pursue it and they walked on, under a small archway that led onto a courtyard. It was pebbled and dotted with young palm trees and the old houses in the mews had all been restored. Daniel led the way towards one of them and raised the large brass knocker.

She was aware of Daniel's eyes on Cosmo and of Cosmo's curious attention on Daniel. It was almost surreal, Alex thought to herself. An hour ago Cosmo had never seen the tall dark stranger standing beside him. And yet now you would think that it was as if they had known each other years.

Ollie answered the door, her small figure lost in a loose-fitting shirt. Emma stood beside her, a dark-haired, elfin-looking little girl, whose big eyes looked up in concern at the visitors.

'Oh, Dr Trent—Dr Hayward, come in,' Ollie said, and smiled down at Cosmo. She led them into a spacious hallway

and then into a long room with a sprawling red sofa.
'Cosmo—Emma, you can go into the garden if you like.'

'Can we play in the summer house, Mummy?' Emma
asked, and her mother nodded.

'Just remember to keep it tidy for Aunty June.'

When the children had disappeared, Ollie nodded to the
sofa and Alex and Daniel sat down. Ollie sank into an easy
chair and pushed her short brown hair from her face. Alex
thought she looked very pale and noticed the bluish rings
under her eyes.

'June's out this afternoon,' Ollie said quickly. 'It's kind of
you both to come.'

'How are you feeling?' Alex asked, though she knew before Ollie replied what the answer would be.

'I'm still getting my head around it all, Dr Trent.' Ollie
paused and drew her shoulders back. 'As you know, that
woman just turned up on my doorstep out of the blue. She
told me she'd been seeing my husband. And she's pregnant
by him.' Ollie drew her hands over her face. 'After twenty
years of what I've always considered to be a happy marriage
I didn't expect something like this to happen.'

There was silence as Ollie fought back the tears, drew a
tissue from her pocket and blew her nose.

'When I last saw you…you were attempting to sort things
out,' Daniel prompted.

'We did,' Ollie replied, adding bitterly, 'And the baby is
Grant's.'

Once again silence enveloped them, until Ollie cleared her
throat and lifted her head. 'I'd convinced myself that Grant
had had a kind of mental blip. A one-night stand, perhaps.
Maybe he'd got drunk or something—a moment of madness.
I don't know. But I certainly wasn't prepared for him to tell
me it was his child and he's in love with her.'

'Do you have any idea what you're going to do?' Daniel
asked.

'I'm trying to take each day as it comes,' Ollie said, tucking her tissue back into her sleeve. 'I'll be in to work to-morrow—'

'You know you can have as much leave as you like,' Alex interrupted her.

'I know, Dr Trent.' Ollie nodded. 'But I'll feel better if I'm doing something constructive. Emma and I are going to stay here for a fortnight. I can't impose on June any longer. I've told Grant that he must decide. But, whatever he chooses to do, that's the end of it. I couldn't take it if he stayed with me and hated every moment. I'd rather him go now and we can both make a clean break.' Her voice broke and she caught her breath. 'He says he still loves me, but he has the baby to think of too. But you can't have it both ways, can you? I mean, he has to choose. For all of our sakes—especially Emma's.'

'Does Emma know what's happening?' Alex asked.

'She understands we're having a holiday here and Daddy is looking after our house. Having said that, I'm certain she senses something's wrong. And I...I have to be strong for her.'

'Are you sleeping?' Daniel asked quietly.

Ollie sat back and stared at them. 'No. Could you give me something? The nights are the worst. My mind just won't shut off.'

Daniel nodded and reached for his case. 'I'll give you something for the short term, which will hopefully get you back into a better sleeping pattern.'

'It's a strange sort of feeling,' Ollie went on vaguely. 'It seems as if it's all happening to someone else.'

Alex knew that Ollie was in shock, and as Daniel cast her a glance she knew that he too was worried for Ollie. He handed her the prescription as the children came running in.

'Mummy, there's a long, shiny snake in the summer house,' Emma squealed. 'Come and see.'

'I think it's an adder,' Cosmo pronounced breathlessly.

'And if they bite you you have to have a syrup, or something, to make you better.'

'A serum.' Daniel grinned. 'But I'll be surprised if it is an adder. They can look quite similar to a grass snake.'

'Oh, dear,' Ollie sighed, and plastered on a smile, catching hold of Emma's small hand. She looked at Daniel. 'Can I enlist your help?'

'Okay, kids, show me where it is,' Daniel said, and nodded to a wastepaper basket in the corner. 'Could I have the use of that?'

Ollie nodded. 'Help yourself, Dr Hayward.'

Alex talked with Ollie as Daniel and the children went into the garden. But they didn't have much time before they all came back. It was a grass snake, as Daniel had thought, and much to the children's delight he had it curled safely in the basket and wrapped in a sack.

'What's going to happen to it?' they both wanted to know, and Daniel explained he would stow it in the boot of the car.

'Can we come with you?' they asked excitedly, and Daniel grinned.

Once again the three of them disappeared and Ollie smiled. 'He's such a nice person,' she murmured. 'I didn't think I could get through that morning, you know. But he told me I would. And that one day I'd look back on it and it wouldn't be so painful.' Ollie looked at Alex. 'You think you know someone—and then, in a matter of moments, there's a stranger facing you. But I still feel Grant will choose us, his family. I have to think that, Dr Trent, or I wouldn't want to go on. We'll pick up the pieces of our marriage together.'

Alex admired Ollie's determination to save her marriage, but she also feared for her. Once *she* had thought, as Ollie did about her husband, that Daniel would never walk out on her. She only hoped that Ollie wouldn't be faced with the same awful scenario and be forced to pick up the pieces alone.

A few minutes later they said goodbye, and as she and

Daniel walked down the lane they were both lost in thought. It was Cosmo who brought them back to the present as he asked Daniel about snakes.

'Did you see poisonous snakes in Africa, Dr Hayward?'

'One or two,' Daniel admitted as they stood by Alex's car.

'What are you going to do with that one in your boot?' Cosmo stared up at him with wide blue eyes.

'Release it in the forest,' Daniel said, and smiled. 'Back into his own habitat. One day British snakes could very well be an endangered species.'

'I wish I could watch.' Cosmo looked up at his mother. 'Couldn't Dr Hayward come home with us and show Grandma? And then we could set the snake free in the garden.'

'I don't think your grandma would welcome the interruption,' Daniel cut in, looking uncomfortably at Alex.

'I bet she would,' Cosmo protested indignantly. 'She loves animals. And—'

'Cosmo,' Alex warned, 'Dr Hayward has other things to do.'

'But the snake has to be let free,' Cosmo said in a small voice. 'We could go through the gate to the forest. And I could tell everyone at school I'd helped with an an...an injured species.'

Daniel began to grin and looked at Alex.

There was nothing she could do, she realised, to stop what was about to happen.

Perhaps there had been, she admitted to herself later, as she drove towards home, with Cosmo sitting in the seat beside her, straining to look out of the back window at Daniel's car following them.

Perhaps she should have said no.

But she hadn't.

And her heart was racing madly.

CHAPTER THREE

HELEN TRENT poured tea and smiled at their guest. 'Alex tells me you've been working abroad, Daniel. Tell me about it.' She placed a cup and saucer on the small table beside him.

Daniel smiled softly, sipped his tea and glanced quickly at Alex. 'Basically, I followed the hunger trail,' he said economically. 'Hunger and privation. Trying to make a contribution medically. Sometimes I couldn't. I just had to watch.'

'Harrowing...' Helen murmured.

Daniel nodded, his grey eyes going over her mother's face with a gentle affection. He began to open up then, and Alex listened, his presence in the room giving her strong waves of *déjà vu*.

Not unexpected, she told herself. He had visited the house frequently all those years ago. They had travelled down from London, eager for the fresh air and intimacy of the New Forest. It had been wonderful. Idyllic, almost. Which was why, she told herself as she watched Daniel sitting in the large easy chair by the fireplace, it felt so strange now.

Nine years. A long time. A hard path for Daniel. And hard for her too. A&E wasn't comparable, but it was cruel and ravaging at times. Seeing life ebb away felt like a failure each time. And after each failure you tried harder when the next casualty arrived. And when there was success and someone pulled through life was sweet. Success was revitalising. The best buzz of all.

They had both tried to make a difference in their own way, she realised. And as she listened to him speak she recalled the younger Daniel, fired with enthusiasm and intensity. Had she been just as intense? she wondered. Nine years hadn't really changed them so much, had it?

'Will you go back?' she heard her mother ask. And she saw hesitation flicker briefly in Daniel's eyes. Unreasonably, something inside her tightened.

'Not easy to answer.' Daniel smiled and glanced at Alex, his eyes meeting hers, then switching quickly back to Helen. 'For the moment I'm enjoying the break.'

'Dr Hayward?' Cosmo bounced into the room, Suzie at heel. 'When are we going to show Grandma the snake?'

Daniel grinned. 'Right now, if you like.'

'I hope I'm ready for this, Cossie,' Helen said frowningly.

'It's not dangerous, Grandma.'

Helen laughed. 'I can assure you, young man, if it was I shouldn't go within half a mile of it.'

'Are you coming, Mummy?' Cosmo linked his hand into Alex's.

'Well—yes…but we mustn't keep Dr Hayward too long.'

Daniel shrugged easily and rose from the chair, his tall frame seeming to fill the room. 'I'm in no rush,' he said, and grinned at Cosmo. 'Let's grab him out of the car, shall we, tiger?'

Alex felt Cosmo's hand draw away and watched the slender little figure dart towards Daniel. They moved together, the tall, lean man and the boy with a mass of fair hair. She gave in to the luxury of drinking them in, then dragged her gaze away as her mother linked her arm through hers—and smiled.

'What is it do you think, Dr Trent?' Jane Glynn looked up from her position on the examination couch and Alex examined the small lump once more. Jane's breasts felt healthy, except for this one area at the bra line, and Alex wanted to be certain of her diagnosis on this thirty-nine-year-old patient. Having recovered from cervical cancer, Jane was right to be prudent about any changes in her body.

'How long has it been there?' Alex asked.

'I suppose about a month. Maybe it was there before and I hadn't noticed. I do check my breasts, but they are lumpy.'

Alex nodded. 'Well, I don't think it's anything to worry about, but I'll get you booked in for a mammography and an appointment with Mr Brace.'

'How long will that take?'

'The appointment won't be long in arriving—I'll ring the department. In the meantime, try not to worry.'

'I can't help it,' Jane said as she slid off the bench and began to redress. 'After the last lot of health problems I really do get anxious. My husband says I was a worrier beforehand, but now it's ridiculous.' She laughed, but Alex knew that she was putting on a brave face.

'We caught the cervical cancer in time,' Alex reassured her. 'There's no reason to suppose this lump is suspect. But, even so, the mammography or scan will show us more.'

'It's the waiting,' Jane sighed as she walked with Alex from the treatment room.

'I know. We'll get you seen as quickly as possible.'

'Thanks, Dr Trent.'

After Jane Glynn had gone, Alex rang through to the hospital and spoke to the consultant's secretary to get Jane's name added to the list.

She admired Jane Glynn, who was indeed a worrier, but rarely wore her heart on her sleeve.

As Alex folded Jane's notes away she heard the sound of Daniel's voice in the corridor. It was unmistakable, a deep, husky tone, raised in soft laughter. Was he about to knock at her door? Her thoughts spiralled to yesterday, and Daniel's visit to the house, to the four of them trundling through the gate at the bottom of the garden and the excitement at the sight of the wastepaper basket's contents.

'He's gorgeous,' Helen had said rapturously, nevertheless keeping a safe distance as the long, shiny body of the snake slithered into the undergrowth. 'Such a lovely colour. A kind of pearly grey-green.'

'We thought he was an adder,' Cosmo pronounced as he hunkered down next to Daniel. 'He's got stripes on his side.'

'The adder has them on his back,' Daniel explained, 'more like tiny black diamonds, really. You'd know one if you saw one, but they are quite rare.'

'It's a shame he couldn't live in the garden,' Cosmo said as the last of the tail disappeared. 'By Grandma's pond.'

'There may be one already,' Daniel suggested. 'In the compost heap or a wall crevice. Or even under tree roots.'

'Can I look, Grandma?' Cosmo pleaded.

'Yes, but be careful,' Helen warned, then turned to Daniel and asked the question that Alex had been dreading. 'Would you like to stay for supper, Daniel?'

Alex's heart had lurched wildly in her chest but Daniel had declined, explaining that he had to call in and see Peter. She'd seen that her son was disappointed to see Daniel go, and her own emotions had been mixed. Just as now, when she heard Daniel's light knock and the sound of his voice in the hall...

A dark head appeared slowly around the open door. 'Are you finished?' he asked as he stepped in. Dressed in a crisp white shirt and dark trousers, he looked oddly formal as he walked towards her, his brow gathered in a frown. She knew before he sat down in the chair by the desk that he was going to tell her about the discussion he'd had with Peter.

'Yes, all done,' she managed, and smiled.

'I've been allotted the room at the end of the passage,' he said, and waited, allowing her time to respond. When she didn't, he added carefully, 'Peter and I decided on three months. If it works out—great...and if it doesn't—well, no harm done.' He paused, slanting an eyebrow. 'You're okay with that?'

'If it's what Peter and Sean want, I've no objection.'

He gazed at her for some while, as through trying to read

her thoughts. His grey eyes moved over her face and eventually he spoke again. 'You have a fantastic family, Alex.' He raised dark eyebrows slightly. 'But then, you must know that.'

'Yes,' she said, and smiled. 'I do.'

'Your son is very much like you,' Daniel continued, 'but then I don't know his father.'

'Zak?' she murmured thoughtfully, wondering how she could possibly describe Zak in just a few minutes. 'Zak is—an extrovert,' she settled for. 'The life and soul of the party. Someone you wouldn't forget in a hurry…'

Daniel nodded slowly and they were silent for a while, until he spoke again, though rather briskly this time. 'I'm sorry if I gatecrashed yesterday. I couldn't really say no to your son.'

'It wasn't your fault,' she assured him. 'Cossie adores animals. I think you've guessed that by now.'

'I share his passion,' Daniel said, and then flicked her a doubtful glance. 'So, about me being here, Alex—'

'It's all right,' she told him. 'Really.'

He frowned then, but finally smiled. 'Well, I'd better let you get on.' He rose, and threw her one last uncertain look, an expression that seemed to melt her inside. Then a smile panned across his lips again. 'Say hello to Cosmo for me.'

She didn't answer, but watched him walk out. Had she answered him honestly? she wondered. She didn't know, and she certainly wasn't going to trawl through it all again. It was enough to know that he would have opted out if she'd asked him. Now the arrangement was made she would make the best of it. Lines, at least, were drawn. It was only her own fear she was fighting—the worst demon of all.

A week later, Alex felt a few vague twinges in her back. Her skiing accident—too stupid for words; a collision with another skier—had resulted in a prolapsed disc. She'd cut her holiday short and hobbled home to a Casualty colleague. The result, as she'd feared, had been bed-rest. Cosmo had gone to stay with her mother, and finally she'd rented out her flat and moved home too.

That was when Peter had suggested, when she felt better, that she do a morning's work at the surgery. She'd been grateful, but had felt no appeal in general practice. She'd been eager to get back to hospital, to resume the demands of her old life.

'Work just one morning,' Peter had cajoled. 'Try it. You might be surprised.'

She had been. The pace was slower and there was time to listen to people. To see an end result, in some cases. And there was more time for herself and Cosmo.

One morning had became two, and crept quickly up to full time. She tried to do justice to her job, and sometimes worked harder and longer than she knew she should.

But as she grew stronger her energy returned, and the weekend had been one of those energetic times. Helen had stayed away with a friend and Alex had gone riding with Cosmo.

She'd mounted an ex-polo pony and defied her back to protest. But on Monday she was stiff and her neck ached. By Tuesday she was feeling ancient. And by Wednesday Peter noticed.

'What have you been up to?' he asked, and she crimsoned.

'I went horse riding with Cosmo. Just a short hack.'

'How long?'

'Oh, an hour or so—'

'More like two.'

She felt herself going redder and Peter wagged a finger.

'You're going home,' he told her, 'to rest.'

She tried, pathetically, to claim it was just stiffness.

'Not a protest more,' he yelled at her. 'Feet up—doctor's orders.'

'I'm just going to collect Cosmo from school—'

'No driving,' Peter ordered.

She crawled to bed that evening and suffered the agonies

of boredom. On Thursday morning there was a knock at the door.

'Peter suggested I call,' Daniel said, his wide, if slightly doubtful smile disarming Alex. 'He doesn't want you in today.'

'But I feel fine,' she argued.

'Would Cosmo like a lift?' Daniel ignored her protest as Cosmo came running down the stairs.

'You can have a rest, Mummy,' Cosmo said, and Alex sighed, decidedly outnumbered.

'I'll return him this afternoon,' Daniel promised.

'I'm not completely helpless,' Alex said, flustered, and helped Cosmo on with his jacket.

'No,' Daniel agreed dryly, 'not quite.'

'How thoughtful,' her mother sighed as she joined Alex at the door and they watched the car slide away.

'I suppose,' Alex mumbled, then wondered, too late, if she looked a wreck. She wore a baggy cardigan and loose trousers and a pair of mules that Suzie had nibbled aggressively. She wasn't wearing a stroke of make-up and her eyes reflected an uncertain blueness under a cascade of blonde hair bundled up on top of her head.

She hadn't even managed a dab of moisturiser. Yet as she glanced in the mirror at the top of the stairs somewhere in her expression she saw something she hadn't seen in a long time. To identify it would have been impossible. But it was there.

Her mother must have noticed too, because she called after her, 'I have to say that Daniel's reappearance in our lives has its advantages. My grandson leaps happily off to school without a murmur of complaint and my daughter looks no more than a schoolgirl herself...'

Alex spent a frustrating, if successful day resting. Peter rang and told her that he didn't want to see her on Friday either, and Daniel returned Cosmo and drove off without calling in.

'We talked about snakes,' Cosmo told them as they ate tea in the conservatory. 'And polar bears!'

Helen raised her eyebrows. 'Don't tell me Dr Hayward has confronted a polar bear too?'

'No, but he's seen brown bears in Canada. There are still some white ones left, but there's not so many as there used to be. They're called injured species.'

'Endangered species,' Helen corrected, with amusement.

Cosmo giggled, then slid a glance at his mother. 'Dr Hayward said he'd collect me in the morning.'

'Did you ask to be collected?' Alex quizzed.

'No.' Cosmo scooped a tail of spaghetti from his chin. 'It just happened.'

Helen hid her smile. 'Very sensible, Cossie.'

'Did you know Dr Hayward before I was born?' Cosmo looked at Alex, his spoon poised above his yoghurt.

'I told you I did, Cossie.' Alex frowned, wondering when and if the hot topic of Daniel would be dropped. 'We were training to become doctors in London.'

'What happened then?' Cosmo asked, blue eyes wide.

'We became doctors. That's all.'

'Oh.' Cosmo studied her carefully. Alex was relieved when her mother asked her grandson about his day in school. A day that seemed peppered with references to Daniel, snakes and polar bears, and very little else.

It was Monday when Alex returned to work, and the waiting room was full when she arrived.

'Flu clinics,' Pauline reminded her as Alex ran her eye over the list on the office desk. 'How's the back, Dr Trent?'

'Great, thanks, Pauline. Enforced rest usually does the trick.' Alex smiled. 'I take it we've notified everyone of the flu clinics?'

Pauline nodded. 'We sent out reminders to those at risk, and we've got two extra nurses in surgery. Sue Peach and Maggie Knight. Maggie's marshalling the queue and Sue is using the treatment room next to Dr Hayward. Oh, incidentally, he asked me to give you this.' Pauline handed over an envelope. 'So—shall we send your first one in?'

Alex nodded and slipped the letter in her pocket. 'Who is it, Pauline?'

'Stephen Hurd. He rang at eight this morning and we squeezed him in. Breathing problems. He doesn't think it's asthma because that usually wears off. But I got him in quickly all the same.'

'Stephen Hurd—the Commoner?'

'Yes—the pony man, my youngster calls him. Lives in one of the cottages just outside Tyllington. He keeps pigs too. All the family are Commoners. A fit lot, usually.'

Alex nodded thoughtfully. 'Give me five minutes and you can send him in, Pauline.'

Once seated at her desk, Alex switched her computer on and slipped the note from her pocket. It was from Daniel, just a few lines, but her pulse began to race as she read.

Cosmo expressed an interest in visiting the wildlife sanctuary in Bedlington. I'm happy to take him, Alex. I've said nothing, of course. But before the weather breaks I thought it might be a small adventure. Daniel.

Alex stared at Daniel's energetic handwriting and her thoughts hurtled back years. With a shiver of awareness she recalled the letters she'd waited for so eagerly. Letters which had always told her how much he missed her. How eager he was to rejoin her in London. But his visits to his parents in the north of England had gradually increased. She'd tried to be patient, to understand his need to help them. And his father had certainly been ill. But it was his mother's demands that had increased, and Daniel had travelled back at every opportunity.

She could still recall the bleak emptiness of the weekends without him. Precious days that had seemed meaningless without his presence. She had hoped separation would unite them. She had believed, right up until that last terrible argument and the ultimatum she'd issued, that he would put their love first.

Alex shivered as she returned to the present. A tall, dark-haired man dressed in a working jacket and cords was standing in the doorway. She wondered how long he had been standing there as he closed the door and took a seat.

'I've got trouble with my breathing,' he explained, in an incredulous tone that suggested he was normally a very fit man. 'Not all the time. Odd attacks that leave me feeling groggy. I'm really mystified as to what it is.'

'Are they connected to anything? Food, exercise, the environment?' Alex studied his handsome weather-beaten features. He was a man in his middle thirties and looked, as he sounded, in the peak of health.

'They started in late August, so my girlfriend tells me. I can't remember exactly, but she seems to think so. What I do remember is that I felt shoddy one night after I came in from putting the breeding sows away. Gail, my girlfriend, suggested I might have an allergy. But I've never had one yet, and my family have been Commoners for three generations.'

'Do you bring your pigs in every night?' Alex asked.

'I have to.' He shrugged. 'That's the deal you get as a Commoner. I can turn them out into the forest all year providing I bring them into my holding at the end of the day.'

'And you've not had trouble breathing before?'

'Not that I recall.'

'How many attacks have you had?'

Stephen Hurd frowned. 'Three, I think. The last one was on Saturday morning. I felt so rough I had to stay in bed. But by the evening it had worn off.'

'Can you describe what happens?'

The big man nodded. 'I get a shortness of breath, a feeling almost of flu—or fever—and a nauseating headache. Damn thing really sends me up the wall.'

'Do you have any irritation of the skin or in the sinuses, watering of eyes?'

'None at all. That's why I don't think it's an allergy.'

By the time Alex had satisfied herself that Stephen Hurd was the healthy young man he appeared to be she was wondering if she was missing something important but totally invisible to her eyes and ears. There was no doubt that her patient's symptoms were real; the problem was locating the cause.

'I'm as fit as a flea, aren't I?' Stephen said as he tugged on his jacket.

'Indeed you are,' Alex agreed, puzzled.

'So where do we go from here?'

'I have an idea,' Alex answered after a pause. 'I'd like you to keep a record of all you do each day. Even the smallest things. And what you eat and drink. When the next attack happens come to see me straight away and bring your notes with you.'

'I'll have a go,' her patient replied gloomily. 'Though I'm not seriously given to diary-writing.'

'Perhaps Gail could help out?' Alex suggested, recalling the mention of a girlfriend.

He looked brighter. 'Yes, you've got a point there.'

After he had gone, Alex wondered if she'd missed something glaringly obvious. But his heart, lungs and reflexes were all working perfectly. He seemed well in all other respects and she was puzzled. He had no history of health problems, so the attacks appeared unconnected to his lifestyle as a Commoner.

Just then a tap came at the door and Ollie Durrant entered. She was carrying a mug and smiled hesitantly as she lowered it to the desk. 'Coffee, Dr Trent.'

'Ollie—thank you—how are you?'

The receptionist bit her lip as she met Alex's concerned gaze. 'Grant moved out on Saturday,' she said, so softly that Alex almost missed it. 'Before we got home from June's.'

'Oh, Ollie, I'm sorry to hear that.'

'I was hoping he would come to his senses, but my big gamble didn't pay off, did it?' She gazed at Alex with tears in her eyes. 'It's Emma who will suffer most, of course.'

'Does she know?' Alex asked gently.

'No. I just said Daddy had gone away on a business trip. Grant wants to speak to her himself. We've arranged that we meet next weekend. I'm absolutely dreading it.'

'Do you really feel like working, Ollie?' Alex said uncertainly. 'Why not take some time off?'

But Ollie only shook her head. 'I want to keep busy,' she said, sniffing back the tears. 'Especially whilst Emma's at school.' She took out a tissue and blew her nose. When she had composed herself she looked at Alex. 'Are you feeling better? One of the girls told me you were off last week.'

'Yes, it was just a small blip.' Alex shrugged, and as Ollie turned to go added quickly, 'If there's anything I can do, Ollie…?'

'Thanks, Dr Trent, but I'll be okay. You and the doctors—and all the staff—have been very supportive. I'll get through this. People do, don't they? And, anyway, there's always a chance that Grant might return.'

How would Ollie cope if Grant stuck to his decision? Alex wondered at odd moments throughout the day. It was tragic to see such a close family break up. And little Emma was so vulnerable. Cosmo had never had the shock of his father leaving him, Alex thought with relief. Zak would have married her, but how long would he have been able to shoulder that responsibility? A year? Two years at the most?

Alex's thoughts returned to the note from Daniel. What was she going to do about it?

It was a question she was still considering by the time she finished her surgery at four. As she walked into Reception Daniel's tall figure appeared in the hall.

'How are you?' he asked, and she nodded.

'Fine. And you?'

'Wondering if I overstepped the mark,' he said, and raised an eyebrow.

'In what way?'

'My note—have you read it?'

'Yes.' Alex smiled. 'But you could have asked me.'

He grinned, a lopsided smile with teeth bared slightly, a slash of white that made her heart swoop. 'I could have, but

I thought better of it. Took the coward's way out. You see, I didn't know what to say to Cosmo. We were just talking on the way to school…about animals, places…and he said that he'd wanted to go on a wildlife trip with his school.'

'Yes—he missed it because he had a cold,' she remembered. 'I promised we would go in summer. But Zak visited and our plans changed.'

Daniel stared at her, his smile fading as he straightened his back. 'Of course. You must have had a full schedule.'

Just then Pauline came along with an elderly gentleman. Daniel began talking to him, gently taking his arm and escorting him back to his room. He gave her a brief smile as he went and she watched them move away, a tang of aftershave snaking seductively into her nostrils.

As she said goodnight to the girls and made her way to the car she wondered what Daniel would think if he knew that Zak's two-week visit had resulted in very little reward for Cosmo.

Zak had taken him to London, deposited the child with his parents and then pursued his own affairs. It was hardly surprising that on their return Cosmo had talked a lot of his grandparents and very little of his father.

An irony that seemed to have reversed itself in the case of Daniel, a stranger in their midst. A stranger of whom her son spoke constantly.

CHAPTER FOUR

'WE SHAN'T be late,' Daniel assured her.

Alex bent to hug Cosmo. 'Have fun, darling.'

'Wouldn't you like to come, Mummy?'

Alex avoided Daniel's gaze. 'I'm taking Grandma to the market.'

'You're welcome to join us,' Daniel said a little formally, but Alex shook her head.

'Thanks, but we've some shopping to do.'

'Shopping's boring,' Cosmo protested, linking his hand through Daniel's as they stood on the doorstep. Both wore jeans and T-shirts, and Daniel's tanned, muscular arm was carrying Cosmo's little fleece.

'Another time, then,' Daniel said politely, his eyes already distanced as he nodded to the car parked outside the gate. 'Let's go, tiger.'

'What shall we see first?' Alex heard Cosmo ask as they walked down the path. 'The bears or the snakes?'

'The big guys?' Daniel suggested, his dark head bent and his broad shoulders swinging, and Cosmo laughed delightedly.

Alex watched them go, her heart squeezing. Cosmo was clearly too excited to pause and wave to her as he clambered inside and the soft purr of the engine drifted them away. Had her son ever reacted this way with his father? Had he ever held Zak's hand and behaved so unselfconsciously as he did with Daniel?

Zak's over-the-top greetings were like the dazzle of a firework. Burning bright one moment, extinguished the next. When the novelty had worn off Cosmo would be left to his

46

own devices, or more often than not, whisked away to London to be amused by his grandparents.

Alex liked Zak's parents. They showed genuine affection for their grandson. She could rely on them to amuse Cosmo and return him safely to her, but Zak knew that too and often took advantage of it.

'Cosmo gone, has he, darling?' Helen came down the stairs, her clear blue eyes meeting her daughter's. The sight of a basket over her arm caused Alex to smile. Her mother had probably been ready for hours.

'Yes—did he say goodbye?'

Helen nodded. 'Oh, yes, and gave me a hug.'

Alex smiled softly, raising her eyebrows. 'Well, this is nice. We've got all day to shop.'

'Hmm,' her mother murmured and, casting her a glance, added a little wistfully, 'Though I'm certain we shan't have quite as much fun as Cossie.'

Alex pulled on a casual jacket and inspected herself in the mirror. 'Why ever not?'

'You should have gone with them, Alex.'

Alex turned and stared at her mother. 'I wasn't invited, not really. It was definitely a boys' thing.' She smiled as she saw Helen's frown. 'And, besides, I don't want to get too involved; you know that.'

'I do,' her mother said softly, 'but, Alex, don't be too quick to judge.'

'I have to, Mum,' Alex answered quickly.' For Cossie's sake as much as my own.'

'I know, Alex. Daniel hurt you once, but that was a long time ago.'

'You sound as if you're on his side,' Alex replied stiffly.

'It's not about sides—' Helen began, but Alex shook her head, the corners of her eyes tingling dangerously.

'Let's take Suzie for a quick walk,' she intervened quickly, only just managing to hide the emotion that threatened to overcome her. 'And then we can make an early start to the market.'

Helen nodded and bent down to attach Suzie's lead to her collar. When she straightened Alex was smiling again. But the incident had made her realise how vulnerable she still felt on the subject of Daniel.

'Cossie! Did you have a good time?'

It was half past six and her son was giving her the bear hug of a lifetime. 'We stayed till they closed,' Cosmo gurgled as she held him in her arms. 'We were nearly the last to leave. And look what we bought!' He pushed away from her and fell to his knees, tugging open his blue and yellow backpack. 'They're videos of all the animals. But the one I liked best is Germaine, the seal,' Cosmo said excitedly as he pulled out his treasures. 'I fed her. They give you gloves and you can throw a fish in the air and she catches it like a dog.'

'How lovely, darling,' Alex said as Daniel hunkered down beside Cosmo on the hall floor.

'And we saw snakes and lizards and a crocodile,' Cosmo rattled on, 'and there's an elephant. And Dr Hayward took some photos and—'

'Cossie…' Alex laughed softly '…slow down.'

Daniel looked up at her. 'Yes, it's getting late. I'd better be going.'

'Will you stay and watch a video?' Cosmo jumped to his feet, his face full of disappointment.

'I don't think so,' Daniel said, his hand lying lightly on the boy's shoulders. 'It's getting late, Cosmo.'

'Can Dr Hayward stay, Mummy? Just to watch a video?'

Alex knew that it was going to be impossible to refuse. At the same time she didn't want the gesture of gratitude to be taken the wrong way.

'I promise I'll go to bed straight afterwards,' Cosmo added, and Alex smiled as she looked at her son.

'You do?'

Cosmo nodded solemnly. Daniel caught her gaze and held it, and she swallowed, glancing quickly away again.

Placing her own hands on Cosmo's shoulders, she looked into serious blue eyes and smoothed the hair from his warm forehead. 'We'll see, but first put your things away whilst I talk to Dr Hayward.'

Her son nodded dutifully and scooted upstairs. She looked at Daniel and met the silver-grey eyes that were studying her curiously. She cleared her throat and said quickly, 'You don't have to stay, of course. I'm sure you're busy.'

'No,' he replied, 'I'm not...but...' He paused then, and for one terrifying moment she though he was going to reach out and draw her against him. Almost every muscle in her body locked as she stood, unable to move. But he shrugged imperceptibly, running his long fingers through his hair, and when she looked into his eyes again she shivered.

She groped for words and pulled herself together. 'You must be hungry.'

'A little.' Daniel nodded.

'Mum cooked lasagna before she went out,' she said in a voice that betrayed the tiniest of wobbles. 'Come through and you can put on the video whilst I make supper.'

Alex turned towards the big reception room and forced her legs towards it. An open fire was burning in the grate and the hidden lights across the room, the huge chintzy sofa and deep, cosy chairs, made the room look inviting. She felt a curl of energy under her ribs as she heard the soft footfall behind her.

Alex deliberately avoided the gaze that followed her as she bent to turn the logs in the grate. It was all she could do to ignore the things it was doing to her body as she looked into the flames. There was no way she was going back on her vow to keep Daniel at arm's length. Just where he should have been nine years before.

They demolished Helen's lasagna, then watched the video. Cosmo curled beside Daniel on the sofa, the warmth of the fire flushing his cheeks. His eyes were a deep, lustrous blue that Alex hadn't seen in a while as he sat absorbed by the antics of Germaine the seal.

She barked and splashed in the water, and her inkwell eyes were as reflectively beautiful as her shiny coat. Involuntarily Daniel's hand snaked out, lay on the back of her son's small neck as they watched.

Alex surveyed them from her single chair, feet curled up, her fair hair scooped behind her ears. She had long since given up trying to watch the video. She was devouring her son, the way he laughed and gazed at Daniel. And Daniel's body language, his deep spontaneous laughter, the strong, protective curve of his arm as it fell to rest lightly behind Cosmo's back.

Then more thoughts came—selfish, unreasonable thoughts— as her gaze lingered on the hard, proud muscles of thighs, the deep, burnished tan of his skin, reminding her that he was a wanderer. An adventurer. A man who had travelled and would travel again.

The video finished and Cosmo yawned. 'I wish we could see it again.' He looked at Alex. 'Is it bedtime?'

Daniel laughed, his body flexing like wire as he moved. Alex saw again the sports-crazy student, the rugby player, the athlete who had taken her breath every time she'd watched him on the field. Such easy, delicious movement, a creature of energy, of power, and yet he'd held her in his arms as gently as a piece of bone china.

'Mummy?' Cosmo's voice brought her back.

'Yes, darling,' she said, standing up quickly. 'It's bedtime now.'

Cosmo launched himself into her arms and hugged her. 'Can I read for ten minutes?'

She nodded. 'I'll come up to say goodnight. Don't forget to say thank you, Cossie.'

Her son went on tiptoe. 'Thank you, Dr Hayward,' he said quietly, and opened his arms. Daniel bent into them.

'It was a great day, tiger.'

When Cosmo had gone upstairs, Daniel said, surprising her, 'I had a fabulous day.'

'I'm glad,' she said. 'Cossie is good company.'

'You've done a wonderful job, Alex. It can't have been easy.'

It hadn't. She'd almost opted out of medicine after Cossie's birth. But she'd fought back and accepted her limitations. Cossie had to come first. He was a darling child and worth the sacrifice of her ambitions. When he'd been old enough for crèche she'd hated leaving him, but she'd also made a decision not to burden Helen with the responsibility. Helen wouldn't have minded, but Alex had been firm for all their sakes. And in the end she had carved out a good life for herself and her son.

'Are you happy?' Daniel asked huskily.

She looked at him, tipping her chin. 'Yes, I am.'

His gaze lingered on her and he said softly, 'You deserve to be.'

'Does it ease your conscience, Daniel?' she said, before she could stop herself.

'Alex, that's unfair.' His face was suddenly carved by lines. 'I always hoped you'd find happiness—the kind I was obviously unable to provide.'

'You had other responsibilities,' she heard herself saying coldly. 'I was well aware of that.'

'None that I couldn't resolve given time,' he answered her. 'I did the best I could under the circumstances—and if—'

'If I hadn't made you choose?'

He looked at her with eyes that were reproachful. 'I didn't want to be away from you.'

She laughed without humour. 'You could have stayed in London after your Finals.'

'I would have,' he told her heavily. 'If you'd given me time to sort things out at home.'

She felt the icy trickle of anger down her spine. 'There's no point in going over it all again, Daniel.'

He looked at her for what seemed an eternity, then nodded slowly. 'Goodnight, Alex. Say goodbye to Cosmo for me.'

She watched him turn and walk across the floor, his tall figure disappearing through the doorway and into the hall. The anger that had made her speak so bitterly suddenly disappeared and she yearned to call him back. To say that the words she had flung at him had not been intended to hurt. She'd hidden the pain so well, dampened it down all these years.

'Oh, Daniel,' she whispered. 'What happened to us?

She heard the front door open, then there was a momentary pause and she thought for a minute he was coming back. But it closed and he was gone.

Her eyes lingered on the sofa, the deep indentation of his body still visible. Alex felt a lump in her throat and swallowed it down. Sentiment had no place in her life now, at least not for the past. And, sliding the video cassette from the machine, she went upstairs to her son.

For the next few days Alex avoided the staffroom, and in the evenings, growing darker now, she took care to leave swiftly rather than stay to talk to the girls.

It was a minor precaution that saved her from unnecessary and embarrassing confrontations. The reception staff were always so busy she was certain they hadn't noticed, and Sean and Peter were either out on calls or had left already.

It was the following Monday that Sean stopped by her room before surgery began and ended her avoidance of Daniel. 'Alex, have you heard?' he asked her hurriedly.

Alex was holding a letter from the hospital and Jane Glynn was on her mind. After a mammography Jane's consultant had advised a biopsy of the lump in her breast, and, though

Jane hadn't made an appointment to see her, Alex wondered how she had taken the news. So it was with a distracted frown that she looked at Sean as he came towards her and sank into the patient's chair.

'You obviously haven't,' he went on, pushing his hair across his forehead. 'I heard it on the local news as I drove in a few minutes ago. There was a fire at the Haven Hotel in the middle of the night and several people have been taken to hospital.'

'I'm sorry to hear that,' Alex replied, aware that Sean was staring at her intently.

'The thing is,' Sean went on hurriedly, 'Daniel hasn't arrived yet.'

Still puzzled, Alex frowned again. 'His surgery doesn't start till ten—'

'I know, but he's usually here by now,' Sean cut in, looking at her anxiously. 'Peter's been trying to get him on his mobile but with no luck. And there's no reply from the Haven, which is understandable.' He paused, then added hesitantly, 'The only other place to look is the hospital. Peter's ringing now.'

'But why should Daniel be at the hospital?' Alex asked as she suddenly began to feel worried.

'Don't you know?' Sean looked at her in alarm. 'Daniel's been staying at the Haven.'

Alex stared at her colleague, trying to make sense of what he'd just told her. With Jane's biopsy on her mind she had been miles away. Daniel staying at the Haven Hotel had no real meaning—until it suddenly occurred to her that she had been so busy trying to block Daniel from her mind that she didn't even know where he was living, where he went home to each night and where he sprang from each morning. It was as though she had tried to ignore his very existence.

'Alex—I'm sorry.' Sean shrugged as he saw her pale. 'I thought everyone knew. He's been trying to find somewhere to rent, but everywhere is still let out in Tyllington.

Understandable for a tourist town like this, I suppose—but damned inconvenient for those who—' He broke off and stood up slowly, leaning across to touch her arm. 'Alex? Are you all right?'

She stood up, her legs shaky beneath her. 'So, do you think Daniel was involved in the fire?' Her voice was barely a whisper.

'Well, we don't know, to be perfectly honest.' Sean sighed. 'The news was brief…' His voice tailed off as Alex tried to control the panic mounting inside her.

'The Haven's quite old, isn't it?' she murmured. 'What? Eighteenth-century—with all those beams and a thatch roof?'

'Yes, I know. Which is probably why it went up so quickly,' Sean said, and then realised his mistake and added swiftly, 'But, as I say, there was nothing on the news about casualties. The emergency services would have got there pretty rapidly. It's on the main road leading into the forest, with the cricket ground in front.'

Just then there were footsteps in the corridor and Peter appeared at the door. 'He's at Tyllington General,' he said quickly. 'They won't say how he is, other than that the fire broke out in the early hours, about four this morning, and he helped evacuate the place and stayed on with the paramedics.'

'So if he was helping the paramedics,' Sean said hopefully, 'he must be all right.'

'Let's hope so.' Peter nodded. 'But he's not being discharged—yet, anyway.'

All three of them were silent and Alex felt her legs buckle. To hide her reaction she sat down again, and with an effort she spoke. 'They wouldn't let you speak to him, Peter?'

'No. But then that's not necessarily a bad sign. They were very busy. Staff had been called from off duty to cope with the burden of casualties.'

'So there were casualties?' Alex felt her voice rise and

Peter nodded, glancing awkwardly at Sean and then back at Alex.

'One of us should try to find out something at the hospital,' Peter said, then looked down at Alex. 'You're down for calls this morning, Alex. There's only four, so Sean and I could make them after our surgeries.'

Alex nodded slowly. 'I'll go straight away.' The thought that Daniel had been in a fire was bad enough, but to think that she hadn't even known where he'd been living was filling her with shame. She had deliberately blocked it from her mind—a point that was now brought home to her as Sean spoke.

'I'm certain he'll be fine,' he said reassuringly, glancing quickly at Alex.

'Yes,' Peter said quietly. 'Let's hope so.'

Alex stood up and reached for her bag. 'And Daniel's patients?'

'I've spoken to Reception,' Peter told her. 'The girls are sorting them out. We'll see emergencies, but I've a feeling most of them will want to rebook. Daniel's made a remarkable impression with his patients...we're very lucky to have him.'

Another fact, Alex accepted, that she had chosen to ignore. And one that now she regretted bitterly. How would she feel if something had happened to him? Her racing pulse and the nausea swimming in the pit of the stomach told her she knew the answer. And she hated herself for it.

'You're...a relative, did you say?' The receptionist at the casualty desk looked harassed as she leafed through her notes. Then, turning to the monitor of her computer, she studied the names and details that flicked up on the screen.

'No, I'm a colleague of someone involved in the fire,' Alex said rapidly, aware of the noise behind her. The small room was buzzing; there were barely enough seats in the hospital's ancient waiting area.

'Oh, you're an antique dealer,' the woman replied, and glanced over Alex's shoulder at a man who was raising his voice in order to be heard. He looked like a journalist and Alex's heart sank as she saw him. Obviously the fire was big enough to create media interest.

'No, I'm not. My colleague and I are both doctors. His name is Hayward—Daniel Hayward—and he was staying at the Haven when the fire broke out.'

'Sorry.' The woman sighed. 'I'll check again.'

'Why did you think I was an antique dealer?' Alex turned to scour the dozens of faces crowding in and out of the waiting area. None of them was Daniel, though she hadn't really expected to see him there.

'It's an annual thing. There's a big sale on Wednesday and the hotel acts as host. Did your colleague come in this morning or in the night?'

'I'm not certain,' Alex said, trying to recall what Peter had said and feeling cross with herself for not remembering.

'There's Dr Miles,' the receptionist said as a door opened along the corridor. 'He's just come on duty—'

Alex didn't wait for her to finish as she saw the white coat vanish. She caught up with Dr Miles as he walked towards Casualty. 'Dr Miles—my name is Dr Trent. I'm trying to locate my colleague, Dr Hayward. He was staying at the Haven and was due to take surgery this morning, but he hasn't shown up—'

'I've just arrived,' the young doctor replied breathlessly. 'But come with me. It's pandemonium out there. The hotel was full, I understand. And unfortunately we're short-staffed.'

This piece of information did nothing to reassure Alex as they hurried down the corridor and pushed through the swing doors. Alex inhaled the familiar aroma of Casualty and scrutinised each of the small curtained cubicles as the staff scurried round the brightly lit ward.

Dr Miles disappeared briefly, then returned with a nurse

at his side. 'Your colleague is in the last cubicle on the left,' she told Alex. 'We're looking for a bed for him, but he's claiming there's nothing wrong and he wants to go.'

'What *is* wrong?' Alex asked, unable to disguise the concern in her voice.

'Go along and see for yourself,' Dr Miles told her. 'I've got an RTA coming in, but I'll try to get back to you.'

Alex watched him dash off, recalling the pressures that accident and emergency doctors and staff were constantly under, but the young nurse remained. 'If you can use some persuasion on your colleague it would be helpful. We really do need to keep him in for obs. The burns aren't so much of a problem, it's the inhalation of smoke. The full extent of the damage might only become apparent later.'

'How much smoke did he inhale?' Alex felt her heart race.

'A bit—apparently he helped the visitors to safety before the emergency services brought him in.'

Alex nodded and promised she would do what she could. Then she made her way towards the cubicle, her heart thudding unbearably.

Daniel sat on a chair beside the bed, naked from the waist up. A swathe of bandage looped across his chest, slicing the forest of ebony hair. Someone had done a pretty good job of cutting off his shirt. She knew that because scissors and a bag were on the bottom shelf of the trolley and one blackened cuff poked out from it.

Alex closed the curtain behind her and took everything in. The painful red welts that spread from fingers to wrists; the careful medical upholstering and empty packets of non-stick sterile dressings.

She hauled her eyes to his face. Her cool vanished as her gaze followed the sutured wound. From temple to jaw it snaked downward, bruised and discoloured under the hospital light. His face had been carefully cleaned, but a blush of smoke lay around his hairline. Other black tails coiled into the well of his neck. His eyes lifted to meet hers in surprise, and suddenly she was moving towards him.

'Daniel… Oh, God. What happened?'

'Alex…what are you doing here?'

'Looking for you.' She came to a halt and didn't know what to do with her hands. In the end they fell uselessly by her sides. She stood there foolishly, torn apart by what she saw.

'Hey…it's all right,' he told her gently. 'I'm fine.'

'You look it.'

He managed a smile at her sarcasm, then asked gruffly, 'Didn't Peter get my message?'

'No. Sean heard the news on the car radio this morning and Peter phoned the hospital but couldn't get much sense out of them. So we decided one of us should come.'

'What happened to my patients?'

'They've been booked again—or Peter saw them. For goodness' sake, Daniel, that's the last thing you should be worried about.'

'I wanted to avoid disruption,' he muttered as she sat down beside him. 'I lost my mobile so I asked one of the nurses to ring in. Obviously she didn't.'

'Maybe she tried, or just had too much to do.' Alex shrugged. 'And anyway, I would have covered for you.'

A rueful eyebrow tracked up. 'You would?'

She tried to ignore the grey eyes that sparkled a soft tease, then, with a sigh, he raised his hands powerlessly. 'You shouldn't have bothered to come, Alex. Really, I'm okay. I just wanted to get myself together.'

'First or second degree?' She nodded at his hands.

'It's barely a blister.' He shrugged. 'For heaven's sake, Alex, don't fuss.'

'I'm not. I'm concerned, that's all.' She couldn't tell him how much. She couldn't say what she had felt when she'd discovered he'd been in the fire. Nor could she reveal how she'd felt when she'd seen him here in the cubicle and her heart had turned over.

He coughed a little and tried to disguise it. Her heart started again, a pounding that tunnelled to her ears.

'How is your breathing?'

'It's okay.'

'Don't lie. A nurse said you helped everyone out of the hotel. The smoke must have been thick.'

'I did what I could. The damn fire sprang up from no-where.'

All the dreadful possibilities tumbled through her mind. The injuries to fire victims that she had treated in Casualty; the lethal effects of smoke that tore at the airways and res-piratory system, blocking the intake of oxygen and boosting levels of carbon monoxide. Pollutants that triggered the im-mune system to go into overdrive and damage the tissues. A chain reaction of poison that could play havoc with the lungs. She had seen it all as a doctor, but now she was on the other side. And it frightened her. Frightened her to desperation.

He looked at her then, and sighed. 'Silly girl. Look at me. It's all superficial.' Slowly he reached out to touch her, but couldn't as he suddenly remembered his injured hands. She looked down at them and swallowed. Then she laid her hand very slowly over his arm. It was all she could do.

'That's nice,' he said huskily. 'Makes being here worth it.'

'Don't be silly,' she chided, her cheeks flushing softly. 'They're trying to find you a bed.'

'They needn't bother,' he grated. 'I told them that.'

'You're crazy. You need assessment.'

'I've assessed myself. I'm dischargeable.'

'To where?' she demanded, outraged. 'Another hotel?'

'Why not? Alex, the others need beds. *Real* casualties.'

'You're not moving,' she told him fiercely, 'until I've spo-ken to someone.'

'Did anyone ever tell you—?'

'How bossy I am?' She nodded as she tugged back the curtain. 'Many times. It comes with the job.'

'Alex—I'm not hanging round here.'

'So you've said.' She nodded again. 'But you're staying in that chair until I'm certain what state your lungs are in.'

He muttered something unmentionable under his breath and leaned back. The hard muscle of his arms flexed and for a moment she almost lost it. He looked so vulnerable, so in need. A powerfully attractive man when in the peak of health, but now, in this precarious condition, her instincts clamoured to hold him, to make him well, to do all that a doctor should do. And more, much more.

'I'll be back,' she murmured, and dragged herself out. She didn't know what she was going to do, but one thing was certain. It was up to her to resolve the problem and decide just where Daniel was going to go.

CHAPTER FIVE

You should think yourself lucky.'

'I know, so everyone keeps telling me.'

'One of the nurses said that two of the casualties they brought in are serious. Daniel, the place could have caved in on you.'

'What was I supposed to do? Walk out? Whistle a happy tune whilst the rest incinerated?'

Alex trained her eyes determinedly ahead, thrust the gear down a slot and growled softly. She wasn't even going to glance at her passenger. Before she had left the hospital, with Daniel reluctantly in her charge, one of the policemen had arrived to take statements from witnesses. He had told her that Daniel had rushed back into what had clearly been an inferno. He'd very nearly been crushed under a beam while he'd dragged out two very inebriated males who had ignored every single warning to abandon the place. She was just too furious to speak.

To think, even!

There had never been such a stubborn individual, such an intractable human being, such a…a…

'Alex?' Daniel's voice came softly.

'What?' She bit her lip, refusing to be mollified.

'You're angry.'

'Too darn right I'm angry. Why didn't you wait for the emergency services?'

'Because I couldn't stand there and watch people be consumed by fire.'

'So you went in to join them?'

'That's childish, Alex.'

'What if the beam had knocked you unconscious? Not just

sliced an inch of skin from your face. What if you'd been asphyxiated or choked or burnt alive? I just can't believe you rushed back into a blazing building!'

'It wasn't blazing, not then. I waited after seeing some women were okay. Then we checked how many guests we had on the lawn. When I saw movement in the bar, two guys trying to open the window—'

'*Then* you rushed in?' she finished for him.

'Alex, I just found a place to get in,' he told her patiently, as if telling a child, 'then I booted the bar door and let them out. Simple as that.'

'Simple?' She glowered at him. 'Look at you—you're a mess!'

'A superficial mess. Give me a week and I'll be right as rain.'

If she replied to that one she might hit him. So she looked back at the road, clenched her teeth, and drove in silence. She knew she was behaving unreasonably. The poor man had saved lives; he was a hero. He had quite coolly prevented a catastrophe and all she could do was nag him. But he could have died in that fire and all he could do was shrug it off.

He hadn't even complained at the hospital—but he had refused to go with her. Luckily Dr Miles wouldn't hear of it. 'Your choice, old man,' the young doctor had told him. 'You know the ropes. You stay here for twenty-four hours or you remain under the eye of your GP.'

'Alex isn't my GP,' Daniel had argued, then had seen the frown on Dr Miles's inscrutable face. 'At least, not officially.'

'So, you're staying in?'

Because he'd had no other option, he had come with her.

She said nothing more as she drove, though she was bursting with outrage. Daniel must have sensed it, because he sat with his dressing-wrapped hands on his knees, his shoulders drooping under a borrowed shirt that was ripped along the sleeves. And tried to hide the side of his face that looked like a pie crust.

Alex had rung home from the hospital and wasn't surprised when she saw Helen waiting for them in the garden. 'Oh, Daniel,' Helen sighed as she opened the little gate. 'You poor lamb.'

'I'm fine.' Daniel repeated his mantra. 'Really.'

'Can I touch here?' Helen curved her palm lightly around his elbow. 'Is it safe?'

Daniel chuckled softly. 'Fire away.'

They were laughing softly at their little joke as they walked towards the house, Helen's hand lying gently under Daniel's arm.

Alex stared after them incredulously. A few words from Helen and Daniel had turned back into a human being again. Now all she had to do was turn back into one herself.

Which had proved, Alex decided that evening, not quite as easy as she'd hoped. She'd gone back to the surgery and given everyone the news, then she'd struggled through her patients and arrived home to find Cosmo barely able to contain his delight.

The story of the fire had reached the school. Some of the children's fathers were firemen and policemen. The news, amazingly, had arrived before the bell had gone.

'Can I tell my friends that Dr Hayward is staying here?' Cosmo asked, having positioned himself next to Daniel at the table.

'It's just for a while,' Daniel told him quickly, glancing at Alex.

'But your hotel's burned down,' Cosmo answered, his gaze fixed on the fork that Daniel attempted to wield. 'How will you get dressed and washed and everything? And you haven't got any clothes. You haven't even got pyjamas. Mine will be too small and Mummy only wears—'

'Cosmo, your supper's getting cold,' Alex intervened quickly. 'And so is Daniel's.'

But it occurred to Alex that Cosmo was streets ahead. Daniel's clothes had been lost in the fire. Luckily his personal possessions and passport were stored in Peter's garage, but as for clothes…

'I could run into Tyllington after taking Cossie to school tomorrow,' Helen said suddenly. 'Pick up a few bits for you, Daniel. I would need your sizes and preference in colour. There's a nice men's shop in the marketplace. I'm certain they could find something to suit.'

'I wish I could come,' Cosmo said wistfully.

'It was only the other day you said shopping was boring,' Alex pointed out.

'I like *some* shopping,' he admitted, after a moment's thought. 'Like going with Grandpa to London. Best of all I like the museum—the one with the dinosaurs.'

Alex felt a pang of regret as she gazed at her son. Cosmo spent so little time with Zak when he came home. She worried about that, but what could she do? She tried to see the positive side, that Cosmo had loving grandparents, but it still troubled her.

It was after Cosmo had gone to bed that Alex realised just how good a job Daniel was doing of disguising his pain—certainly from the burns on his hands. Though Dr Miles had assured her he had seen to it that Daniel had pain relief, and the medication they had brought home was substantial, it was the cough that worried her most.

'I'm in the room next door,' Alex told him as they said goodnight. 'So if you need me—'

'I know where you are,' he said, and jerked an eyebrow.

'There's a bathrobe behind the door,' she continued, ignoring his expression.

'Helen showed me earlier.'

'Can I help you wash?'

'Thanks—' he grinned '—but the nurses did a pretty good job. Maybe I'll shower tomorrow.'

'You'll have to cover those wounds—' she began, but his rueful smile stopped her.

'I think I'll be able to manage.'

Blushing, she pushed open the door. The bed had been turned down by Helen and a soft glow filled the room. A pile of fluffy white towels lay on the damask chair beside the double bed. 'Will you sleep, do you think?' Alex asked anxiously.

'Like a log. Please don't worry, Alex.'

'I'll come in before I leave tomorrow,' she promised him. 'And if you cough—'

'I'll be fine,' he interrupted her again.

Her heart went out to him. His borrowed shirt looked crumpled and his beautiful grey eyes were hollowed by tiredness. One side of his face was still swollen around the sutures and she knew that it would not be an easy night.

'Are you still cross with me?' he asked her softly.

'I should be.'

'But you're not.' He bent down to her slowly, his good cheek lying gently against her face. She could feel the warmth of his hands resting above her shoulders as he held them in mid-air, unable to touch her. Her arms yearned to respond, to take him against her and to hold him. She almost gave in, feeling tiny shudders run between them, a heat that was nothing to do with his wounds.

Her eyelids fluttered down. She swallowed and crazy thoughts flew through her mind. Memories, sensations, little gems of pleasure that were linked to the past and came hurtling back. Then desire rocked through her, no idle threat, but a need that had no place in her life right now. A need that, thankfully, was just pure fantasy. Never more so than now, when physically she couldn't even touch him, let alone…

'Alex…?'

She flicked open her eyes and found him gazing at her. 'Yes?'

'I'm grateful,' he whispered, and kissed her, slowly and softly, as every muscle in her body melted under his lips. 'That was just a thank-you,' he murmured huskily. 'I've nothing else to give you.'

She swallowed as he lifted his face, and wondered how she was going to leave him. But leave him she did, escaping across the thick blue pile of the carpet to close the bedroom door behind her.

Her dreams were more than vivid. They were shamelessly erotic.

Probably because he was sleeping in the room next door in the big double bed, wearing practically nothing except that bandage across his chest. Not that she had the remotest chance of walking in there to find his long, lean body tussled in the white sheets, making his deep tan seem like an apparition.

No, that image was reserved for her dreams, followed closely by another. She was bending over him, uncurling the bandage, but before her fingers had looped the last little bit over his shoulder her touch had healed the red flush of anger beneath. And soon the dressings had fallen from his fingers too. She was lying beside him, the dream magic working so rapidly she really believed she was making love to him—until she woke in the middle of the night, swathed in dampness.

She remained awake for hours then, and hauled herself from bed very early. Refusing to be the victim of her dreams, she made toast and coffee and took it up to his room. She tapped softly, not wanting to disturb either Helen or Cosmo. When he didn't reply she went in, expecting to find him asleep.

But the bed was empty, the covers strewn back. The sound of water came from the *en suite* bathroom. She set the tray down and walked towards the gurgling, her heart starting to beat fast. Her eyes lingered on the shower door. But all she could see was a fine mist that streaked the glass. 'Daniel? Are you coping?' she called, and the rush of water stopped.

Guiltily, she stepped back into the bedroom—and waited. Cymbals crashed in her head. They seemed in some way connected with her dreams and quickly she pushed back the ridiculous notion.

It was a little while before Daniel appeared, a towel draped around his waist. His naked body was steaming.

'You've showered?' she asked shakily.

'Couldn't sleep.' He shrugged lightly. 'So I went downstairs to the kitchen. Found some plastic bags and a couple of rubber bands to cover my hands. It's amazing what a little creativity will do.'

His chest bore a fresh dressing, squared by white tape. He must have changed it somehow. The cumbersome bandage of her dreams had disappeared. She felt a moment's irrational disappointment, then pulled herself together. Whatever was she thinking?

'Your eye looks rather black,' she said, and hesitated. 'How does your cheek feel?'

'A little sore. But I'll live.'

'There's a towelling robe in the bathroom,' she added unnecessarily, her eyes remaining as long as was decently possible on the tall, sleek shape that had suffered no change over nine years. More honed, sleeker, maybe, with an abdomen that looked cast-iron, soft drops of water gliding down the ski slope ripple of muscle.

'I know. You told me last night.' He nodded. 'And Helen left these—a little on the small side, but they'll do nicely.' Daniel looked down the long, wet plane of his calves to the mules on his feet.

'Oh…yes.' Alex hesitated, slightly thrown at the sight. 'They're Zak's—he probably forgot to pack them.' They were a pair no doubt carelessly discarded under the bed or chair during his summer stay and retrieved by Helen.

Daniel looked at her, then nodded slowly. 'Of course.'

'You seem to have managed without my help,' she murmured, trying to think what she should do next.

'Not at all,' Daniel said quietly. 'You came to my rescue yesterday. I'm in your debt, Alex.' He moved slowly towards her.

'I…I'd better wake Cosmo,' she stammered.

'Alex?' His eyes were the soft, luxurious grey that did such terrible things to her insides.

'I'm touched that you were so concerned. I realise you were angry with me because you cared.'

'We were all concerned, Daniel,' she answered stiffly, and made herself open the door. 'Eat your breakfast and try to rest. We can talk tonight about what you want to do.'

She left quickly, not going to Cosmo's room but to the kitchen. It was a quarter past six, still early. So she made a fresh cup of coffee and gulped it down. Dreaming of Daniel was one thing, but going in and seeing him like that…

Thank goodness, he was only staying for a short while. He'd been perfectly correct, of course. She did care. Much more than she wanted to admit.

They didn't get around to talking, not properly anyway. Because they were one doctor short at the practice her surgeries were extended.

Daniel complained that he felt useless and was fit to come back, but Peter took one look at his hands and refused point blank.

'A couple of weeks,' he told Daniel firmly. 'Then we'll work you till you drop.'

So Daniel was forced to comply. It was clear he wouldn't even have been able to use his computer properly, let alone examine someone. Besides, the gruesome little cough still niggled and Alex was worried about it.

'We can go shopping for your things,' Helen suggested, but of course he couldn't drive and had to settle for being a compliant passenger. They bought clothes and shaving things, and books and magazines, and several pairs of shoes. Then he prowled restlessly, waiting until Cosmo came home.

Daniel began to help with homework. He read books and was read to, and Alex marvelled at the change in him. And not only in Daniel, but Cosmo too. When prep was over they'd hare off to the garden and creep round like conspirators. Cosmo would gingerly lift rocks and logs and he and Daniel studied the busy world beneath.

Then there were field trips to the forest. Helen packed them sandwiches and a flask, and with Suzie at their heels they would disappear through the gate, not to be seen again till dark. Unmentionable specimens were set free in the pond as Suzie watched, ears pricked, and at night she would lie by Daniel's feet, her nose against the heel of his shoe.

Meals were hilarious. Daniel's antics with cutlery became his party piece. It was only when Alex realised he could almost grip his fork and knife properly that she knew that soon they'd have to sort out when and where he was going.

It was a week after the fire when Martin Glynn came to see her. He had been very supportive to Jane, his wife, throughout her cancer, but as he walked in Alex guessed that it was not good news.

'Jane doesn't know I'm here,' he admitted at once, and drew a letter from his pocket. He handed it to Alex. 'Read this.'

She read the letter from Jane's consultant and looked at Martin. 'This letter is addressed to Jane,' she told him carefully.

'I know. I opened it this morning by mistake.'

Alex said nothing, though she glanced at her notes and saw that Jane's mammography had been in September. Since then she had been advised to have a biopsy. Alex had thought

it strange that Jane hadn't contacted her, and there had been
no news from the hospital. As she looked at Martin she wondered why Jane hadn't told him.

'Jane didn't tell me about this,' her husband said anxiously. 'And by that you can see she hasn't gone to the hospital to have any treatment. Jane's missed her appointment
with Mr Brace—the consultant at the hospital.'

'Have you spoken to Jane about this?' Alex asked.

'No, she's at work. It's my day off. I phoned your receptionist and she fitted me in. I was so worried—after all that's
happened…and then not knowing about this…'

'Martin, I'm afraid I can't discuss Jane's medical details,'
Alex said gently. 'But I'm sure if there's a reason for her not
discussing this with you it's a very valid one.'

'Has she got cancer again?' The question came unexpect-
edly and Alex realised he was distraught. Before she could
reply, he leaned forward and tears filled his eyes. 'I rang the
hospital. They wouldn't tell me, even though I'm her husband. We've been through so much in the last two years…'
Then, as though he knew that she was unable to answer his
questions, he slowly sank back in the seat and buried his face
in his hands.

'Martin…come on, this isn't like you.' Alex stood up,
fished a couple of tissues from the box and went round to
lay her hand on his shoulder. After a while he used a tissue,
drew a hand across his forehead and with red, raw eyes
looked up. 'I'm sorry,' he apologised.

'Don't be. You're worried, and sometimes it all gets too
much, doesn't it?'

'I…I don't want to lose her, Dr Trent. I can't even think
of living without her. I've never said this before—always
pretended that everything will be all right—but when I read
this I just lost it—why couldn't she confide in me?'

'I don't know, Martin. But she would be devastated to see
you like this.'

'I've never told her how much I worry, because she's a

worrier too and there's no use both of us looking on the bleak side. I've always tried to be strong for her.'

'And you have. But you two must tell each other how you really feel.'

'I thought we did. This thing is a bolt out of the blue.'

'Why don't you ring Jane and ask her to come home?'

'To be honest, I don't trust myself to speak—and anyway, what would I say? Even if she didn't want to tell me, why didn't she go to her biopsy appointment?'

Alex didn't have an answer for him, but it was clear he was suffering from shock. 'Shall I ring Jane on your behalf?' she asked, and he nodded.

'I'd appreciate that, Dr Trent.'

He gave her the number, and Alex called Jane and explained that Martin had arrived at surgery. She tried to say it in a way that wouldn't cause her alarm. Without disclosing why she hadn't told her husband, Jane said that she would speak to her boss and drive straight over.

'She's coming,' Alex told him as she replaced the phone. 'You can use the little room at the end. Ollie will make you both a drink, and when you've sorted things through come back in to see me. I'll answer any questions I can.'

When Ollie had taken Martin to the room at the end of the hallway she came back in and Alex explained the situation. 'Could you slot the Glynns in again?' she asked Ollie. 'No doubt it won't be for a while.'

'Okay,' Ollie said. 'Though it might overlap a bit if I tack them on to the end of surgery.'

'That's fine, Ollie.' Alex smiled. 'How are you? How are things at home?'

'Oh, all right.'

'No news?' Alex asked tactfully.

'No, none.'

'How's Emma?'

'I don't really know, Dr Trent,' Ollie admitted on a sigh. 'She won't talk to me.'

'Is there anything I can do?'

'I wish there was,' Ollie replied with an effort. 'I'm sure it's just going to take time…getting used to the idea that Daddy isn't living with us any more. He told her that weekend, as he said he wanted to. He said that he'd met someone else he liked as much as Mummy and he was going to live with her. That Emma could go and see him whenever she wanted. That he hadn't stopped loving her—or me—but he loved someone else as well. He didn't mention the baby.' Ollie's voice shook for a moment, then she continued, 'Emma didn't cry or anything. But she didn't say anything afterwards either—didn't ask any questions. Just went to her room and played with her toys.'

'Have you explained your side of things?' Alex asked. 'How Grant's decision to leave home has affected you?'

'No, not really. Grant said he wanted to be the one to tell her and I went along with him. But every time I try to bring the subject up with Emma she makes it clear she's not interested.'

Alex nodded thoughtfully. 'Well, I'm sure, as you say, it's just going to take some time.'

Ollie shrugged quickly. 'Anyway, life goes on.' She opened the door. 'I'll take Mrs Glynn down to the treatment room as soon as she arrives.'

'Thanks, Ollie.'

When she was on her own again, Alex thought about Emma. She was such a bright little spark, with so much character. It was tragic to see a family split up, yet there was no going back. Ollie would have to assume both parental roles for a while, and Emma would have to accept the changes in her life that her parents' actions had brought about.

Later, Jane and Martin returned, and it was clear they had talked through the problem. They were holding hands as they sat down and Martin was composed, though Jane looked exhausted.

'I should have told Martin,' she admitted heavily. 'I don't know why I didn't. I think I just wanted it all to go away.'

'So you haven't seen Mr Brace?' Alex asked in concern.

Jane looked down at her knees. 'No.'

'Jane, you do realise how important this biopsy is?'

'We do, Dr Trent.' Martin nodded, and slid a glance at his wife. 'It's just that…well, this time…it's more difficult…'

'Even more reason to have it,' Alex said quietly. 'As with your cervical cancer, a microscopic examination of the tissue will give the correct diagnosis and we can act swiftly—if needs be.'

'You mean remove the breast if the tumour is malignant,' Jane said sharply, and stiffened, her eyes wide as she looked at Alex. 'Well, this time I don't want to know. I've made my decision.'

'But, Jane, you can't do that,' Martin said incredulously.

'I can, Martin. I'm not having the biopsy.'

'But why?'

'Because I can't go through it all again. I can't do it, Martin. I've had enough.' Jane stood up and turned slowly to Alex. 'Please don't try to change my mind, Dr Trent. As far as the lump is concerned, that's all it is—a lump.'

'Jane—' Alex began, but the young woman had walked to the door. Her husband followed, half turning back before hurrying after her, a look of bewilderment on his face.

Alex sat for a while, unable to believe what she had just heard. It happened sometimes that patients refused to be helped, but with Jane being the worrier she was, this was a complete behaviour reversal. Not only that, but Martin was obviously very distressed too.

There was nothing that could be done, though—at least for the moment. After surgery she would think about it in the hope that inspiration would strike. The one road she didn't want to go down was the one that would upset Jane most. Attempting to make her see reason—reason that she had completely blanked out.

That evening, when she arrived home, a taxi drew up at the same time. Daniel's tall figure climbed out of it and she saw his hands were free of dressings.

'Daniel, your hands,' she heard herself saying incredulously.

He lifted them slowly. The red flashes and cracked skin were still there, but he flexed his fingers. 'Not bad, eh?'

'When did they take off the dressings?'

'Outpatients this afternoon. It was fine; I just need to keep out of trouble for a few more days until they've hardened up. There should be very little scarring.'

'Should they be exposed so quickly?'

'Just as long as I take care,' he said, and, looking at her from under dark lashes, added, 'I asked about those two casualties—the ones that were serious and had to be transferred to a special burns unit. They're both going to make it.'

'Thanks to you,' she said quietly.

'No, I was just lucky to be there,' he muttered, and before she could answer he said in a low voice, 'Alex, now that I'm on the mend I must go. There's no excuse to burden you any longer.'

She wasn't prepared for the way she felt then. She hadn't prepared for the sinking sensation that made her legs feel like cotton wool. Or the wave of desperation that washed over her, the powerlessness that brought it clearly home that she didn't want Daniel to go. She had grown used to him being around, being part of the family, to hearing his laughter and sometimes his cursing, and most of all, just knowing he was near.

Oh, God, she thought helplessly. What am I going to do now?

CHAPTER SIX

THE one thing she tried not to do was panic. So she told herself that Daniel's leaving was all for the best. What would it be like if he stayed a month, or two—or more? For Cosmo, the wrench would be impossible. And it was with that thought that she tried to put life back into perspective.

It wasn't made easy for her. The following day at work Peter asked her how Daniel was.

'Improving,' Alex told him. 'Where the beam hit him on the face is healing nicely. The scar's a bit ragged. But it'll heal. And the black eye has completely gone. So,' she ended wistfully, 'he's really quite good.'

Peter perched on the edge of the office desk, one eyebrow arched. 'What about the cough? He's not still hacking, is he?'

'It seems better.' She nodded. 'And he hasn't complained.'

'Well, the man wouldn't, would he?' Peter peered at her. 'But he needs to stay off another week. You must make him.'

'I can't, Peter. He's a doctor, for goodness' sake.'

'Which makes absolutely no difference at all. Can't you use a little charm and persuasion?'

'Even that won't wash,' Alex admitted. 'He wants to move on, Peter.'

He looked at her for a while, before standing up and walking slowly around the desk. When he drummed his fingers on the top of it, and then gazed up at the ceiling, Alex knew an idea was brewing.

'I was wondering,' he murmured, his gaze glued to the ceiling, 'about Terry Hall's place…'

Alex frowned. 'The photographer?'

'Yes. His place backs on to the forest. Not far from your mother's. Got a huge swimming pool. Colourful chap.'

'I have heard tales,' Alex said dryly. 'But why do you mention him?'

'I met him at a charity bash last year and he took some pretty fantastic photos of Virginia and the kids. We've had him round to dinner a couple of times and we've been round there.'

'To one of his famous parties?'

Peter chuckled. 'No such luck. He doesn't stay at the house for more than a few months before he's off again. It was just a thought—he might well like a housesitter and Daniel might fit the bill. Someone reliable—honest—trustworthy…'

'Well, yes, I suppose… But—'

'I could have a word,' Peter murmured nonchalantly.

'I think you'd better speak to Daniel first,' Alex said quickly. 'I've no idea what his plans are.' The words hadn't slipped from her mouth before she saw a smile form on Peter's lips. If she didn't know better, she would have thought her colleague had already been doing some homework of his own. But she decided to say nothing about Peter's idea. It might fizzle out altogether.

It was on Friday that she had a telephone call from Stephen Hurd the Commoner who had been in some weeks before. He was short of breath and feeling ill. Alex told him to rest until she got there. She had finished surgery so she told the girls at Reception where she was off to and drove there straight away. She was greeted by his girlfriend, Gail, who had just arrived back from holiday.

'I've just got here,' she told Alex as she led the way through the low-beamed rooms. 'And he tells me he's been like this since Wednesday, the idiot. I was uncertain about going away and leaving him and I was right.'

'How long have you been away?' Alex asked as they made their way past rows of boots and outdoor clothing that had the distinct aroma of pig manure. It was strangely pleasant, though, and Alex wondered who was taking care of the animals. But before she could ask Gail had unlatched one of the stable doors along a stone-paved passage and was leading the way into a rather gloomy bedroom.

'Dr Trent's here, Stephen,' she said as they approached the bed. 'And she'll tell you what I told you, I expect. You should have phoned the doctor earlier.'

'Got to get the pigs in,' he muttered as Alex sat on the bed.

'I'll do it,' Gail said, and sighed. 'Just stay where you are before you fall over again and hurt yourself.'

In a glance Alex could see that Stephen Hurd was unwell. She unravelled him from the sheets and as she began to examine him she had to agree with Gail: half-delirious and with a raging fever, there was no way he was going to get up and see to his pigs.

'I've got to,' Stephen protested, trying to throw off the covers. 'Got to get out—'

'Stay still, Stephen, please.' Gail pushed him gently back as Alex listened to his chest. The abnormal sounds that ricocheted through the stethoscope confirmed her suspicions that he certainly couldn't stay at home.

'I'm going to admit him to hospital,' Alex decided quickly. 'I don't like the sound of his chest and he can't breathe properly. The sooner we get him in, the sooner we can find out what the trouble is.'

By the time Gail had organised some clothes and an overnight bag the ambulance had arrived.

'I'll have to stay and see to the animals,' she told the paramedics, 'but I'll be in later to see him.'

'I asked Stephen to keep a diary,' Alex said as the ambulance waited. 'It would help if I could send it in with him. Might give them a clue as to what's going on.'

'I wrote it for him.' Gail nodded. 'And I made him promise to keep it whilst I was away. I'll have a look on the desk.'

'What does it look like?' Alex asked.

'It's a blue exercise book with teastains on the front—just

like the rest of Steve's stuff—totally wrecked.' She laughed shortly. 'Though he keeps his barn spotless.'

They searched everywhere after the ambulance had gone, but the diary was nowhere to be found. 'It's useless,' Gail said eventually, slumping down in a chair.

'Could we look in the other rooms?' Alex asked, though she was beginning to wonder herself.

'Help yourself.' Gail shrugged. 'There's two bedrooms and the loo and the kitchen, all full of junk.'

Alex looked askance at the chaos. 'I'll just have a quick look.'

'I'd like to help, but I have to get the animals sorted,' Gail said, rising wearily to her feet. '

'Okay,' Alex agreed. 'Gail—I don't suppose you have any idea what triggered off the attack.'

'Search me. Steve's priorities are his pigs and his ponies. He's hardly likely to suddenly catch a fever from them, is he?'

'No, I can't see that he should,' agreed Alex, puzzled.

'Dr Trent—there's something…' The young woman bit her lip and stopped, then gave a brief shrug. 'It doesn't matter. Nothing important.'

And Alex watched her curiously as she pushed her feet into huge green wellies and trudged outside.

Alex searched whilst Gail was rounding up the animals, but she found nothing that resembled the book. Eventually she phoned the hospital and enquired after her patient.

They told her that they had given him oxygen and put him on a ventilator and he was now able to breathe. After assessment he was being sent up to a ward. When Gail returned Alex told her and they had another look for the diary. After half an hour they gave up and Gail made a cup of tea in the kitchen.

'I'm going to the hospital tonight,' she said as they drank. 'If he's feeling better I'll ask Steve what he did with it.'

'They said he was comfortable.' Alex finished her cup of tea. 'Let's hope the tests will give us some idea of the cause.'

'What sort of tests?' Gail asked, looking anxious.

'All sorts, I expect,' Alex replied, then frowned. 'Why?'

'Oh, nothing. I just wondered.'

Alex had a sense of unease as she got up to go, and did something she would not normally have done. 'Gail, here's my mobile number. Ring me if you find the diary, will you?' She scribbled her number and handed it over.

'Are you sure? It's the weekend.'

'I'm on call until tomorrow evening. But I could pop over on Sunday and help you search again.'

Despite Gail's reluctance to take the number, she did, and Alex left.

She'd half expected Gail to phone that night, but it wasn't until the following morning, as Alex was about to go down to breakfast, that her mobile rang.

'It's all going pear-shaped,' she heard Gail say. 'Stephen says he hasn't seen the diary but promises that he updated it. Added to which he's creating a dreadful fuss. He's worried about his pigs and ponies. He's trying to leave hospital and he looks awful.'

'Have they done any tests yet?' Alex asked quickly.

'No. They haven't had the chance. Oh—here he is now...'

'Dr Trent?' Stephen's voice was gruff and he had a faint wheeze. 'Whatever it was that affected me has worn off. I'm on my feet again.'

'I think you should stay for tests—' Alex warned, but was interrupted once more.

'I can't leave Gail to do all the work,' he protested. 'It's just not on.'

'Haven't you got someone who can step in for you?'

'No one that knows all my animals. They'll only come for me or Gail. And I can't have her trekking about the forest all night.'

'What do you do about holidays?' Alex asked in surprise.

'I used to have another Commoner to help me out. A mate who lived up by Marl. But he's moved out of the district now and I haven't found anyone I can trust enough yet to take his place. It's no easy job, Dr Trent, trying to find and herd in your pigs and ponies that have scattered for miles.'

'Well, there must be someone—' Alex began, but stopped as she heard shuffling noises on the line.

'He's gone,' Gail said, then, obviously upset, 'I'll have to go after him.' And the line went dead.

Alex sighed and snapped the phone back on her belt, but before she could move it rang again. The on-call centre that the surgery was linked to asked her to visit an elderly lady with chest pains. She dragged on her coat and didn't manage breakfast, saying a hurried goodbye to Cosmo and Helen. Daniel made no appearance. Making her first visit, she admitted the elderly woman with chest pains to hospital.

The calls came thick and fast throughout the day, and it was only when she was on her way home that she had time to think about Stephen and Gail again. She almost turned towards the cottage, but decided against it. Gail would no doubt ring her as she had her mobile number. And anyway, perhaps it was best to let the dust settle before confronting Stephen again.

The house was quiet when she went in, and, walking into the big front room, she found Daniel standing by the TV. He was wearing jeans and a rugby shirt and had a screwdriver poised awkwardly over a plug. 'Before you ask—' he grinned darkly '—I'm mending the fuse. At least, trying to.'

'How far have you got?' She slipped off her coat and sank onto the sofa, watching him as he tried to twist the screwdriver. 'Can I help?'

He waggled his fingers in the air. 'They won't do as they're told yet. But I think I've managed.'

'Poor things,' she commiserated. 'They're still growing skin.'

He pushed the plug in and the TV chanted loudly. 'Bingo!'

he exclaimed joyfully. 'I'll never take mending a fuse for granted again.'

'Congratulations.'

He zapped off the set and ambled across the floor. 'Hungry?'

'Not specially. Is Mum in the kitchen?'

'No. She's taken Cossie out.'

Alex closed her eyes. 'Oh, heck. I forgot. It's the school theatre production, isn't it? When did they leave?'

'About half an hour ago.'

She groaned and checked her watch. 'Six o'clock. Why did they leave so early?'

'Helen met Ollie in Tyllington this morning and said she'd call for Ollie and Emma to save taking two cars. She said they wouldn't be late and not to worry that you couldn't make it.'

'How could I have forgotten?' Alex muttered grimly.

'Something to do with you working all day?' he teased.

'At least it'll be nice for Emma,' she murmured. 'From what Ollie's told me, she's been rather withdrawn.'

'Come on,' Daniel said, and caught her arm. 'Tell me all about it whilst we eat.'

She went with him to the kitchen and gasped in surprise at the stacked breakfast bar. 'Did my mother leave all that for us?'

'As they say on the TV shows, I just threw a few things together. A little green salad, pasta, a few herbs, mayo and rice—and *voilà*!'

'*You* made all this?' Alex wriggled onto the bar stool. 'But how did you manage with your hands?'

'Helen invested in some kitchen gloves for me. She's very thoughtful.'

'I know,' Alex sighed. 'Which makes me feel even guiltier.'

'About me being here?'

'Of course not you.' Alex pouted. 'About me—and Cossie.

She has her own life and Cossie and I have taken up too much of it. Mum's young enough—'

'To meet someone?' Daniel suggested, and spooned the food onto her plate.

Alex shrugged. 'Why not? She's still very attractive.'

Daniel raised an eyebrow, hiked himself up on the stool and leaned an arm on the bar. 'So what will you do when you leave here?'

The question came as a surprise and she hesitated. 'I told you. I'm going back to A&E.'

'You're certain?' he queried with a frown.

'Why shouldn't I be? Before my accident I was enjoying my career—' She broke off and narrowed her eyes. 'Daniel, is this some kind of third degree?'

'Did you ever think your accident might have been fate?'

'No.' She laughed softly. 'Next you'll be saying it was a tree that stepped out in front of me as I went down a slope.'

'Maybe the tree knew something you didn't?' he posed, and his smile faded. 'I'm just trying to work out why you want to fix something that's not broken. You have a job you're made for, a great relationship with your mother, and Cossie loves it here. Apart from a few minor glitches, like being unable to get to one or two social events, your life seems remarkably balanced.'

Alex shook her head a little, as if to clear her mind. 'Daniel, you don't understand.'

'Then make me.'

She spluttered, raising her hands. 'I...I...need to reclaim some independence. To get back to hospital life. General practice is...is...'

'Is *you*,' he said quietly. 'You're a wonderful doctor. Totally committed to your patients—you were even prepared to haul yourself out to help find that blessed diary. You're desperate to give Ollie support and you're frustrated because you can't talk some sense into Jane Glynn. Now, tell me truthfully, haven't I just described the perfect person for general practice?'

She met his challenging stare, then sighed. 'You don't understand,' she muttered again, and got up to clear the dishes.

'What don't I understand?'

'Oh—nothing. Forget it.' She knew he was watching her, so she kept her back to him and fiddled with the percolator. 'Coffee in the other room?'

'Okay.' He came up behind her and whispered, 'Sorry. I should mind my own business.'

She tipped in the coffee and flipped down the lid. 'I do have an agenda, you know, even though it might seem obscure,' she said in a hurt little voice. 'Just as you have yours, Daniel.'

He gave a little grunt of acknowledgement and moved away. Why had she snapped at him like that? Had he probed too much? Somewhere close to the truth? No, ridiculous even to think of it. And she hurried up the coffee, hoping the subject was closed.

They took their coffee in beside the fire, and she slipped off her shoes and tucked her feet up under her on the sofa.

'I wonder if they're enjoying the play,' she mused.

'You bet,' Daniel said as he sank beside her and looped an arm along the cushions.

She slid a careful glance his way. How swiftly the wound on his cheek had healed. In a month or two you'd practically see nothing, and he hadn't coughed all evening. The glow from the fire flickered on his face and her heart gave a little spurt. She didn't want to argue with him. He really didn't understand, but only because she couldn't tell him. She couldn't say how vulnerable she felt, how uncertain.

And all since he had appeared in Peter's room that day. Before, she had known her path in life, been confident to take it. But now Daniel had made her question everything.

He looked at her and she smiled. 'What?'

'Cossie's having a ball—you'll see.'

She smiled faintly. 'I should be grateful.'

'But you're not?'

'I hate leaving outings to Mum,' she faltered. 'It's unfair.'

'You can't do it all, Alex.'

'I don't do enough. It's so easy living here. Mum fits in—and I let her. And yet I know I have to move on, to make our lives work again. My back's almost better, and I—oh, I'm just tired, I suppose. And filthy.' She pushed her hands over her face. 'I need to shower and pamper myself. Then I won't feel so ratty.'

'Rattiness,' he murmured, then dipped his fingers into her hair. 'Now, what can we do for rattiness?'

Her heart bounced and bumped at his touch and she sat very still. The movement of his fingers continued mysteriously over her scalp. A little trickle went down her back, like an icicle sliding down her spine.

'Close your eyes,' he told her, and she closed them and very nearly drowned in the twisting and tugging he was doing.

When she couldn't hold her breath any longer, she let it out slowly and mumbled, 'Your fingers. You've already been fighting with fuses. And pasta.'

'This isn't fighting,' he said, and pulled her against him. 'It's relief for rattiness.'

'I don't want to hurt your chest,' she complained. 'Is it still sore?'

'No. And even if it was your head's on the other side.'

Lying still, against his chest, wasn't just mesmerising, it was heaven. She could feel his smooth breathing, the rise and fall of his ribcage. She loved having her scalp massaged, though she couldn't think how long ago it had last happened. Probably, she thought in horror, it was when she had last curled up like this.

With Daniel.

Almost a decade ago…

She'd had no close relationship with a man since then. A few dates, a fleeting romance with Cosmo's father. And then there hadn't been room for commitment. There was Cosmo and her job—in that order. And she had been determined to let nothing intrude on them.

But now, after all these years, it was happening again. What he was doing wasn't just soothing. It was sexy and sensual and her skin was aflame. She knew she shouldn't let him continue. If she had any backbone at all she'd stop it right now.

'Better?' he whispered after a while.

She moved a little. 'Shall I get up?'

His hands ran down slowly to her shoulders as she lifted her head. 'Alex?'

She was frozen. She wanted to move but she couldn't. She didn't want to be anywhere else on earth. She just wanted this…

'Alex, look at me.' He slid her shoulders around so that her arm went up to his shoulder and his gaze lowered. 'Alex…this feels so good…'

'I know.'

'And I don't trust myself—'

'You don't…?'

'So—maybe…maybe we should move…'

'Yes. Maybe we should…'

But neither of them did. Instead, he tilted her chin and kissed her mouth, and that was the beginning of the end. The end of any token resistance she might tell herself she had. Which she didn't, of course. She wanted this kiss so much, yearned for his arms around her and his breath on her face. All of her was missing and wanting, in this split second. All the hurt and loneliness that she'd smothered brought her back here, to this moment.

His warm lips opened and invited her in, the sweetness so perfect she responded at once, her hands slipping round his neck, fingers tussling deliriously in his hair. It had grown longer, she realised, the short crop of spikes now a thick glossy cap of burnished black that felt gorgeously sexy under her touch.

Her small cry of surprise was trapped in her throat as she registered what was happening. The chemistry was as explosive as ever—more so, probably—as he drew her against him, sliding her sideways so that she lay in his arms, his thighs pressed hard against her hips. She gave another little moan. She didn't need to get any closer to know what was happening to him, and as his tongue thrust deeply into her mouth and teased her teeth both became aware of his arousal.

Not that she could disguise her own as his fingers slid over her blouse to the swell of her breast. She shuddered as he traced the growing peak, so gently that she realised he still had to be careful of his fingers and her heart gave a little pang of sympathy. Then suddenly he groaned, deeply this time, as though fighting within himself, and clasped her with a catch in his throat. One hand slipped down into the waist of her skirt and fumbled with her top.

She felt as though she was on a train, a runaway, that there was nothing she could do to stop it, and her heart pounded as he tugged out the cotton and delved against her skin.

She tried to think what she was doing, gasping as he bit her lips gently, moaning softly into her hair and neck. She couldn't let it go on; she couldn't. But she wanted him so much, and deep down desire pooled again, threateningly, maddeningly. Then his fingers were fighting with the clasp of her bra and she arched instinctively against him. A movement that she realised caused him to growl and curse a little as he met real resistance when the clip grazed his poor fingers.

He cursed softly, and something about that sound made her open her eyes. Flushed and dark-eyed, he was staring at her. She saw desperation and desire mingled in them—and something else—a stranger, the grown-up man and not the boy she remembered.

'They still hurt, don't they?' she whispered, and he held her, his hands uselessly cupping her back as she rested on his knees.

'No...'

'Don't fib,' she told him gently.

'Alex?' She winced a little as he brushed the hair from her eyes. His finger traced across her cheek. 'I'm leaving tomorrow.'

'Tomorrow?' she repeated foolishly, the word trembling on her kiss-bruised lips.

'Peter's fixed things up with a friend of his—a photographer,' he told her slowly. 'I wanted to tell you when you came in, but...' He fought for words and shrugged his shoulders.

Then his hands dropped away and she lifted herself, tucking in her blouse.

Easing herself back against the sofa, she took a resigned breath. 'You were going anyway.'

'You and Helen have done so much for me.' He reached for her hand and squeezed it as much as he could, and she smiled bravely.

She made herself meet his eyes. It came back in a rush then—the way she'd felt as he was kissing her, the need, the impossible yearning for the one thing that she couldn't have. She couldn't have Daniel, her first love, her soulmate. That Daniel had gone for ever. This was Daniel the traveller, the man who had passed through many people's lives as he would pass through hers.

A flash of light flickered into the room. 'They're back,' she said, and looked at him again, this time with eyes that were steady. 'Don't tell Cossie tonight,' she said quietly. 'Wait till tomorrow.'

With a small sigh he nodded, and glanced at her again, his eyes too dark to reveal what he was thinking. And then the front door opened and Cossie burst in, rushing to tell them his news. As he leapt up to Daniel his beautiful blue eyes were full of wonder, and Alex's heart tightened.

CHAPTER SEVEN

'I COULD use some help moving in,' Daniel told Alex early next morning. 'May I borrow Cossie for the day?'

She knew it was really an offer to soften the blow for Cossie, and so she agreed.

He left with Daniel after breakfast and the house seemed deserted after they'd gone.

'How quiet it is without them,' Helen mused as they cleared the breakfast things. 'At least Terry Hall's isn't far. I walk Suzie past the bottom of his garden.'

'You liked having him around, didn't you, Mum?' Alex busily piled the dishes into the washer.

'Yes, darling. Didn't you?'

'It was good for Cossie...'

Helen stood thoughtfully. 'It was different with Daniel, somehow.'

'You mean...different to when Zak stays?'

Helen smiled reflectively. 'I suppose I do.'

'Let's have coffee and then take Suzie for a walk,' Alex said, efficiently sliding a cloth over the worktop. 'It's a gorgeous morning.'

'In other words, subject closed,' Helen murmured, and cast a wry glance at her daughter as she reached for the lead on a peg by the door. 'Come on, Suzie, where are you?'

But Suzie didn't bound into the kitchen as usual, so Alex went in search of her. She found the dog sitting by the front door, waiting for Daniel to return, her nose to the crack.

It wasn't just her mother's dog who seemed to have withdrawal symptoms. Alex had them too. Suzie didn't help, each day nosing her way into the guest room to sniff the bed. And it was the following Thursday evening when Helen and Suzie came hurrying up the garden path at dusk.

'I saw Daniel,' Helen said breathlessly as she took off her coat.

'Where?' Cosmo asked, looking up from his prep.

'In the garden of the house,' Helen said, and slanted a glance at Alex. 'I waved and he saw me. He asked me if I had a few minutes to stop—and I said I had—'

'Did you see the swimming pool, Grandma?' Cosmo interrupted excitedly. 'Isn't it humongous?'

'Well, I just caught a glimpse, darling. But it was the house that surprised me the most.'

'You went inside?' Alex narrowed her eyes.

'It's a brilliant house for hiding in, isn't it, Grandma?' Cossie came to stand by Helen. 'I helped Daniel take his things up that big staircase. There are hundreds of rooms. You can nearly get lost.'

Helen smiled and looked at Alex. 'That's true. There are so many corridors—'

'You went upstairs?' Alex widened her eyes.

'Daniel wanted to show me Terry Hall's photographs,' Helen explained. 'They really are stunning, and quite moving. You should see them, Alex. In fact, Daniel said he would be happy to show you.'

Alex hid a sigh. 'I'm sure he was just being polite, and anyway—'

'Yes, dear, I know your feelings on the subject,' Helen said diplomatically as she laid her hands on her grandson's shoulders and wheeled him back towards his prep. 'Come along, Cossie, show me what you've been doing.'

A smile touched Alex's lips. She wondered if Daniel had voluntarily made the suggestion she go to see the photographs, or had her mother, with her quiet charm, made it impossible for him not to?

The week had passed without any news from Gail or Stephen Hurd, and as Alex prepared to start her Friday morning surgery she wondered if Gail had found the missing diary. There was no guarantee, Alex decided, that it would reveal a clue. Stephen might not even have made entries in it, and maybe had even thrown it away.

Not that his attitude had helped at the hospital. Unless he agreed to tests he'd risk another attack. There was no way around the problem as far as she could see. Stephen would have to make arrangements for his animals. Despite his misgivings that no one else could supervise them, no one was indispensable.

Which was not quite the case with Jane Glynn, whose health was also at risk. But in this instance Alex knew that Jane's fear of a biopsy was founded in her previous cancer. And yet, without the investigations that were so necessary, Alex was stumped.

Just as she was about to ring through for her first patient there was a knock at the door and Daniel poked his head in.

Alex licked her lips, the tip of her tongue flicking over them nervously. 'Hello, Daniel.'

He looked gorgeous in a sea-island-blue cotton shirt and dark chinos. Grey eyes glimmered under lazy hoods and a thick ebony fringe of lashes beat down against his cheeks. His scar was barely noticeable and his hands hung easily at his sides. Something wonderful drifted across the desk and she inhaled. The scent was deadly enough to send her pulse racing again. He was just too good-looking for this time in the morning. No, she corrected herself despairingly, for *any* time of the day.

Was it just a week ago that she had lain in his arms, wanting him to make love to her? That his arms had held her and his breath had shimmered over her face? And if her mother and Cosmo hadn't come home...

'Alex?'

She started. 'Sorry. What?'

He smiled slowly, crookedly. 'Did Helen mention yesterday?'

'That she saw you…yes.'

He waited, as if hoping she might speak again, and when she didn't he shot her a frown. 'Did Helen say I showed her the house?'

Alex nodded. 'She told me about the photos.'

He moved forward, then stood still. 'You should come and see them, Alex. Can you drop by on Sunday?'

She shook her head hesitantly. 'I don't know…'

'The photos are from all over the world. Terry Hall's exhibiting them in London before Christmas, so they'll be gone in a couple of weeks. Seems a shame to miss the opportunity.'

'I'll think about it, Daniel.'

'Okay. Let me know.' He turned and, sliding her one slow and unforgivably gorgeous smile, he left. She was left with his scent in her nostrils and she kept smelling it all day long. It even followed her into the car that evening, and all the way home.

On Sunday she found herself alone; Helen had gone to church and Cossie was riding with his friend Marcus. A gymkhana was to be organised by their riding school, and Marcus's mother had collected Cosmo after breakfast.

Alex wondered about Daniel's offer, her hand reaching out for the phone. She drew it back again. She would love to see the photographs, of course. And she probably wouldn't have the opportunity again. But a small voice inside whispered that it wasn't the photographs she was most interested in seeing.

Eventually, curiosity—she called it that to ease her conscience—got the better of her. She changed into jeans and a warm sweater and bundled her hair under a baseball cap. Suzie barked madly when Alex led her into the forest, as though sensing where she was going. The October sunshine shone on the path and her sneakers crackled on the fallen leaves. By the time they arrived at the garden the sun was filling the afternoon with a soft golden light.

Alex paused at the gate and peered in, but the garden was deserted.

For a while she gazed in silent admiration at the sprawling timber-framed house. The modern extension seemed strangely at odds, but it worked somehow, and she wondered how anyone could stay away for very long from such a beautiful home.

There were no lights on, nor did the garden reveal any movement. Then suddenly she saw Daniel, his tall figure emerging from the side of the house. Suzie barked as she saw him through the wooden struts of the gate and he raised his hand to wave.

Like her, he wore jeans and a dark sweater, and his hair was brushed damply to one side, as though he'd just showered. As he came closer the silver-grey pools of his eyes melted against the tan of his skin and a smile widened his full mouth. He drew back the bolt on the gate and she stepped in.

Suzie made her usual fuss and he threw her a stick that she had refused to part with. Then he looked up, smiled again, and Alex felt the bittersweet wonder of being in his company again.

'I'm sorry I didn't let you know I was coming,' she said quickly, to hide her confusion. 'It was a spur-of-the-moment decision.'

'I'm glad you came,' he told her quietly, and hiked an eyebrow. 'Where's Cossie?'

'Riding, with a friend.'

'Then it's just you and me.' He held out his hand and turned his palm. 'Do you see? Pretty good, aren't they?'

She smiled and laid her fingertips gently on the warm, soft skin. 'Remarkable,' she said, and looked up to meet his eyes.

'Come on, then,' he told her, and folded her hand into his. 'Be prepared to be surprised. This house is something else.'

* * *

It was more than a house, Alex realised, it was an experience. Terry Hall's idea of home comforts was unusual.

The ground floor had been revamped from its original Victorian décor. The big rooms were simple and spacious and the furniture ultra-modern. But, like the extension built on to the house, it seemed to work.

They put Suzie comfortably in the utility room and Daniel led the way to the hall. 'There's a lab and a darkroom upstairs.' Daniel nodded to a modern, spiral staircase. 'And a gallery. Besides any number of bedrooms.'

'It's breathtaking,' Alex sighed. 'Cossie said you could get lost here.'

Daniel chuckled. 'He liked the pool, but it's covered for the winter.'

Alex raised an eyebrow. 'Did you meet Terry Hall?'

'No—his agent, who knows Peter. He seemed happy enough with who I was. But to tell you the truth when I saw the place I was a bit doubtful.'

'Why?' Alex looked at him in surprise.

'The place is alarmed from top to bottom.' He grimaced. 'Evil things, in my opinion, but necessary. Along here…the first door of the extension.'

Alex followed Daniel into another passage and realised she was already lost. There were modern pieces of sculpture that looked incredibly valuable, and when Daniel opened a door to their right she gasped in surprise.

'This is amazing, Daniel.' She glanced down a long room whose walls were filled with photographs. In the middle, running down the bleached white boards of the floor, was a bench. It travelled the length of the room and was obviously there for the viewer.

They walked slowly down the aisle and Alex took a breath. There were portraits of celebrities and aristocracy and Alex moved incredulously along the line of the rich and famous.

'I can see why Helen was impressed,' she said, and Daniel smiled.

'I think she was. But more so by these…'

They turned to the next aisle, where the mood and subject changed. These were black-and-white photographs of Third World countries and Alex sat quietly on the bench to look at them.

'It breaks your heart,' she murmured, 'to see such poverty.'

'Perhaps we aren't reminded enough,' Daniel replied as he sat beside her.

'How can we let it happen, Daniel?' she sighed. 'When we have so much.'

'Maybe we can only do what we can.'

'You've been there,' she said quietly, and turned to look at him. 'And you'll go back, won't you?'

He stared for a long while ahead of him, then said quietly, 'When I see stuff like this I feel as though I should. That I'm wasting time…'

She tried to ignore the pang of dismay at his words. In her heart she had known from the beginning that he would leave again. The experiences he had endured had made him the man he was and she couldn't expect it to be different.

But, yes, she had hoped—selfishly—that it might.

'Come on,' he said, and cleared his throat. 'Let's see the rest.'

They stood and went on, and the theme changed again. These were lighter and funnier, wonderfully poignant: children and animals and the photographer's own sense of fun and quirkiness captured in them.

But when it was over Alex was relieved. The room contained so many emotions, and not least were her own. It was a gentle reminder that Daniel would pass through and be gone again from her life.

'Coffee?' he suggested as they walked down the staircase. 'Or a glass of wine?'

She shook her head. 'Cossie will be back from riding soon.'

They stood in the impressive hall, the long, slim window cleverly shedding light into all corners. 'It really is an amazing place,' she said softly.

'I guess I'll be happy to rattle round for a while.' He shrugged. 'But a home has to have a certain ingredient. Like your little flat in London—remember?'

She laughed and caught her breath. She met his eyes and wondered if he was remembering the long hot nights spent in her ridiculous single bed, with the window wide open and the noise of someone's stereo drowning out the traffic beneath. They would lie cramped and uncomfortable and blissfully happy, and after making love take strawberries and wine onto the roof garden. And stare up at the stars and wish that tomorrow was a million light years away.

Yes, she remembered their love-nest, and it hurt.

'Can I walk you back?' Daniel was asking, and she nodded.

'Alex—'

'I'll get Suzie,' she said quickly, and moved away. She didn't want him to see into her mind or guess the thoughts she was thinking. Instead she made a great fuss of Suzie, then clipped on her lead and walked back to Daniel with a bright smile. And told herself that she was being very sensible for not stopping—even though Cossie wasn't due back for ages.

Julie Dingle was a sweet girl, Alex thought as she listened to her young patient's complaints, but at twenty-six seemed to have more than her fair share of problems. Their last consultation had achieved very little, Julie was explaining. And, added to her recent problems, she had become depressed and irritable.

'I feel too sick to take the painkillers you prescribed,' Julie said, and heaved a sigh. 'And the migraines keep getting worse.'

'Do you still work with a computer?' Alex asked.

'Yes. I haven't been able to cut down my hours either. And then there's my fiancé, who says it's all in my mind. We argue all the time and I really just feel like ending our engagement. I'm not even sure if I want to get married. Sometimes I don't think Tim and I are right for each other.' She looked under her lashes and blushed. 'He never really gets, well…you know, turned on.'

Alex wondered if the pretty auburn-haired girl sitting in front of her really did want to change her life. They had discussed her unsuitable job and her lifestyle before, and now it was her fiancé, Tim.

'Let's take one thing at a time,' Alex said, and glanced at the notes. 'We whittled down the headaches to stress. You were going to look for another job.'

'I did. There's nothing.'

'Nothing at all?'

'Nothing I like. Really. There's nothing in Tyllington except shop work.'

'And you don't want that?'

Julie looked startled. 'It's dreadful money. I can't live on less. I mean, could you go from being a doctor to shop work?'

Alex sat back and smiled. 'I'm not unhappy in my job, Julie. But you are.'

'I don't want to jump from the frying pan into the fire.'

Alex trapped her lip thoughtfully. 'All right, set the job aside for a moment. Why do you feel your boyfriend isn't turned on?'

Julie look surprised. 'Because I keep getting migraines.'

'Are you sure?' Alex raised her eyebrows.

'Of course I'm sure. He's said so. He says I'm imagining them to get out of sex.'

Alex paused. 'Is there any truth in that?'

'Of course there isn't!' Julie rose to her feet, her pink cheeks flaming. 'You've got a nerve, Dr Trent. All I want is something to help my migraines that doesn't make me sick, and you go on about me going off sex.'

'No, Julie. That's not what I said.'

'I've never once said no to him—even when I've felt really awful. I've just let him—well, do what he wants, and I don't complain even when it hurts—'

'Julie, sit down—please. I'm on your side. I'm trying to help. If I've touched on a sensitive subject then I'm sorry. But maybe because the subject is sensitive we need to discuss it.'

Her young patient sniffed and sank slowly down on the chair. Alex gave her time to recover and wondered how she should tackle the subject again. Julie had consulted her three times this year, but nothing seemed to have helped the migraine problem.

'How long have you been engaged?' Alex asked quietly.

'A year…on and off.'

'Because of the quarrels?'

Julie nodded. 'We just go round in circles.'

'Julie…you said you don't complain, even when it hurts? When you make love, does it hurt?'

Without looking at Alex she nodded. 'I have a headache and feel sick, and going to bed is the last thing I want to do. Except to lie in the dark and have some relief from the splitting headache.'

'Have you talked to Tim about your job?'

'No, because he would say I could easily get another one. Just like you did.'

'I didn't exactly say that. I just pointed out that I was happy with my job but that you don't appear to be with yours. However, let's try to look at the important issue. Your relationship with Tim.'

Julie looked up and frowned. 'But my migraine is the most important issue.'

Alex said nothing for a moment, until Julie blinked. 'You think I'm so focused on my headaches—?'

'That your engagement has become less important? It's possible.'

'But I do love Tim,' Julie protested earnestly. 'It's just that sex is uncomfortable.'

Alex put down her pen and stood up. 'Well, let's make certain that you've nothing to be concerned about. Hop up on the bench and we'll check.'

'Is that necessary?' Julie asked doubtfully.

'I see by your records you're having regular smears, and they're fine. When I've examined you we'll be able to eliminate any other concerns.'

Julie finally agreed, and though she was tense Alex was able to complete her examination. Julie dressed again and sat by the desk, pushing back her hair and licking her dry lips. 'So, what do you think?' she asked anxiously.

'I think you're a very healthy young woman. But you're inclined to become tense. Your muscles tighten and that would make sexual intercourse less pleasurable. It's quite common, Julie, and getting to the underlying cause always helps. Now we've discussed this we can tackle the headaches.'

'I still don't see how headaches are caused by sex,' Julie said truculently.

'They aren't. They may be a referred pain—from anxiety, stress, pressure, all sorts of things. It doesn't help if you can't let go for a while. We all need to let off steam—even doctors,' Alex added ruefully.

Julie smiled then, and they laughed, and Alex knew this wasn't going to be another one of those unfulfilling consultations. 'Which of our nurses does your smears?' she asked.

'The little one—Sue, is it?'

'Sue Peach. I'll make an appointment for you. She runs a clinic and has lots of info on how to relax—and some brilliant videos.'

'You mean on sex?'

'On all aspects of relationships, Julie.'

'God, Tim will think I've gone potty if I tell him the doctor gave me sex videos to cure my migraines.'

Alex laughed softly. 'You've nothing to lose. You might as well give it a try.'

Julie sighed, then giggled. 'Oh, well, why not?'

'Go to the desk. I'll tell the girls to fit you in.'

Julie smiled as she rose. 'Today hasn't been quite what I expected, but there you go. Thanks Dr Trent.'

Alex watched Julie leave, then rang through and told Reception. The appointment was made and she tucked Julie's notes back into order. Alex couldn't resist a smile. The last ten minutes could have swung either way, and Julie had almost walked out. It had been worth digging a little.

Then her smile faded as she realised something else. She had admitted to Julie that she was happy in her job—a small concession and one that was unimportant to Julie. But it came as almost a surprise to Alex. She *was* happy here. She *did* love her job.

Which was exactly the opposite of what she had told Daniel. And, most importantly, it was the opposite of what she had been telling herself.

A week after her conversation with Julie Dingle Alex was still thinking about her little admission. It had niggled at the corners of her mind ever since. And, much as she tried to conjour up pangs of missing her old life, they just didn't seem to materialise.

Almost without her knowing, she'd become involved in general practice. She did love this job. And it wasn't what she had expected.

In the mornings, as she drove to work and dropped Cosmo at school, she thought about it a lot. General practice had got into her blood. She had thought nothing could replace the frenetic buzz of Casualty, the brief, triumphant moments of the emergency room and the dip of emotions at the other end of the scale. But practice life had wormed its way into her consciousness—the mysterious channelling of a connection between doctor and patient that grew over time.

The union had to be nurtured and preserved, and it wasn't all happy endings—not by a long shot. Some patients were intractable, refused to be helped, and some were downright rude. But they were in the minority. Most of them were genuinely in need of help and worked at helping themselves.

General practice had become addictive, she realised. And she didn't know how to react. Had Daniel sensed it when he'd talked about trying to understand her motives? If he had, he'd not brought it up again. But the response she had given to Julie had made her think. And think hard.

A week later, as she hurried across the car park, muffled up in a scarf and warm coat against the first sharp frost of the month, Daniel caught up with her.

She turned at the sound of feet crunching over the autumn leaves. The conviction that had sustained her for so long about returning to hospital had been shuffled away somewhere, and when she looked at Daniel she felt almost guilty.

Not that he had the slightest inkling of what she was thinking. And why should he? His thoughts were in another direction entirely. She'd known that for certain since going to Terry Hall's house and seeing the photographs.

'Alex—slow down a moment. I've been trying to catch you all week.'

She looked at him in the melting October evening and felt her heart speed. He wore a heavy coat with its collar turned up, and his breath curled in the cold air. A rosy glow filled the sky, but the trees were almost a luminous gold. The colours were breathtaking, and his eyes seemed to reflect them as they met her gaze.

They began walking together towards the cars and she wondered what it was that was so urgent.

'There's a bonfire in Tyllington soon. Would Cossie like to go?'

'I hadn't thought that far ahead,' she said hesitantly. She'd had some vague idea of setting off a few fireworks in the garden. But Suzie was nervous of loud bangs and Helen wasn't keen on the idea. She'd suggested instead they have Emma and Marcus round for Hallowe'en.

'It was just a thought,' Daniel murmured doubtfully. 'Anyway—see you tomorrow.' He began to walk away.

'Daniel?' she called out, and followed him. 'I'm sure he would—thanks.'

'What made you change your mind?' He walked back towards her.

'I hadn't made it up. It's just that my mother wasn't sure about fireworks because of Suzie, and I think we settled for a kids' party on Hallowe'en.'

'Great—what time should I arrive?'

She laughed, and then shrugged. 'Come if you like.'

'I was only joking.'

'I know, but the offer's there. And…' She paused and frowned up at him in the darkness. 'Thank you for the offer of the bonfire. Is it a school night?'

'No, they've arranged it for the Saturday.'

'Well, I can't see why Cossie shouldn't go.'

'We'll talk about it again,' he said easily, and then raised his hand. 'Oh, I had a patient today who you know. Martin Glynn.'

'Jane's husband?'

'Yes. One very anxious man.'

Alex sighed. 'Because of Jane?'

'They're having a very hard time of it. I rather had the impression that he would have preferred to see you, but there wasn't an appointment free so the girls gave him to me. I've signed him off work.'

'He's ill?'

'I'm not certain. I gave him a full examination and palpated all round, but I couldn't find any painful areas. He said it's been painful below his chest. I thought perhaps it might be a slow case of appendicitis, or even pleurisy—I was a hair's breadth from sending him to hospital.'

'What stopped you?'

'I told him to rest and to let me know immediately if he develops pain over the next twenty-four hours. I've made another appointment for him on Monday, but my guess is I'll be seeing him before that.'

'Could it be herpes zoster?' Alex guessed.

Daniel paused. 'He's only forty, but it's a distinct possibility.'

'He's had a lot of stress. Did he say if Jane's changed her mind?'

'No. And I didn't ask.'

Alex nodded and dredged up a smile. 'Keep me posted, won't you?'

'Of course—and about that party—are you serious?'

Alex grinned. 'If you're game, yes.'

Daniel nodded slowly, a smile spreading over his lips. 'Hallowe'en.... Trick or treat—or maybe the arrival of an unexpected stranger? I'll see what I can do.'

But am I letting you do too much? Alex wondered as she said goodnight and unlocked her car. Glimpsing his dipped headlights in the driving mirror, she preferred not to answer that question.

CHAPTER EIGHT

'CAN I have another jelly, Alex?'

'Of course you can, Emma. Come on, let's fight our way to the table, shall we?' Alex folded her hand around the smaller one and led the way through a gaggle of screaming, laughing and tumbling children in the drawing room, through to the hall and into the kitchen.

Alex had been concerned about the little girl when she'd first arrived. Grant—Ollie's estranged husband and Emma's father—had dropped her off. It was the first time Alex had met him since the split. Ollie had mentioned at work that he would be bringing their daughter and Alex had wondered if his new partner would be with him. But he'd come at five o'clock alone with Emma and asked what time he was to collect her. As it was Saturday Alex had said eight, since none of the children would have to get up for school.

'Here you are—strawberry or orange?'

'Strawberry, please.'

'One strawberry coming up.' Alex squeezed the plastic container into Emma's hand. 'Do you want anything else, darling?'

'No, thank you. When is my daddy coming?'

'When the party ends at eight.'

'I'm staying at his house tonight.'

Alex smiled. 'That will be fun.'

Emma looked down at her jelly. She was such a pretty little girl, with soft, long-lashed dark eyes and a sweet mouth, but there was something distanced about her that hadn't been there before the break-up of her parents' marriage. 'I don't think I'll be going to stay again, though,' she said with a hitch in her voice.

103

'Why is that?' Alex asked in concern.

Emma looked up and bit her lip. 'My daddy is having a new baby. There won't be room for me.'

Just then Helen poked her head around the kitchen door. 'Pass the parcel, Emma. Are you playing?'

Emma nodded and placed her jelly back on the table. 'I'll eat it afterwards.'

Alex watched her go and was still staring after her when there was a tap on the kitchen door. She opened it and Daniel grinned at her from under a large black hat. 'It's the best I could find,' he said, and stepped in, hauling a sack with him. 'But I think wizards' hats should have stars and moons and things on, shouldn't they?'

Alex closed the door. 'It's brilliant. Where did you get it?'

'A gift shop in town. The woman who owns it sorted these pressies for me.' He opened the sack. 'I explained it was for a kids' party and her husband rummaged in the storeroom and found the sack. Rather effective, don't you think?'

Alex peeked inside. 'Bats…lizards…spiders—oh, Daniel, wonderful. They'll love them.'

'Nice little critters, aren't they?'

'Wait a moment. I've got something else.' She rushed upstairs, rummaged in a chest of drawers and dragged out a creased, but perfectly respectable black cloak.

'They won't run away from me, will they?' Daniel asked doubtfully as she draped it round his shoulders.

'Hardly. You make a spectacular wizard.'

And he did. A little trail of excitement shivered down her spine as she gazed at him. His beautiful grey eyes glimmered mysteriously under the peak of the hat and the black sweater and jeans he was wearing went perfectly with the cloak. He gave her an uncertain smile. 'Are you sure?' he asked with a straight face. 'This is my first time.'

She laughed. 'You'd never know it.'

He shot her a frown at the noise in the other room. There

was laughter and a lot of cheering. 'How many of them are in there?'

'Eight. But they're all very good little children,' she teased. 'They haven't turned us into frogs or cream cakes so far.'

'I'm relieved to hear it.' He gave her a very unwizardly leer. 'Though you look delicious enough to eat.' She had thrown on a long black dress from the same chest as the cloak and gelled out her hair with green spikes. Even Cossie had been impressed. Now Daniel was staring at her with one eyebrow hitched. 'I've always wondered what it would feel like to cast a spell,' he murmured as he reached out and drew the cloak around her. 'Maybe tonight I might find out.'

Something in her chest felt as though it was about to snap; it could be panic, or anticipation, she thought desperately; or it could be something much more lustful.

'Hmm, so where should I begin?' he muttered theatrically, warming to his theme. 'I'd better get a bit of practice before I go in there…'

His head came down and his arms enfolded her as a rumble escaped from his throat and she laughed. But then, locked in his arms, she made no movement, her fingertips poised on his chest as he clutched her against him. She found herself wondering if the thick black forest of hair had recovered after the fire, and whether or not it would be easy to run her fingers through the tight little whorls.

Then suddenly her eyes locked with his and they weren't laughing any more. She fumbled her fingers under the cloak and stopped over the base of his neck. He felt warm and strong and wonderfully sexy. 'Don't you have to say something about bats' wings and frogs' legs…?' she began, and swallowed.

'Something like that,' he said huskily, his mouth coming down slowly. For a moment she could hardly breathe as his tongue flicked over the contours of her lips and the smooth blue lipgloss that tasted faintly of plums. Then his arms went round her more tightly and his tongue slipped into her mouth. She prayed that Helen would keep the children busy. That none of them would rush in and discover a witch and a wizard kissing...

But no one came in, and suddenly they were kissing and tumbling against the table and heat seared between them like fire. He saved them—just—from falling, and propped her against the wall, his hands going round her waist and fixing her there as she let out a little cry of surprise.

'Daniel... We mustn't...'

'I know we mustn't.' But he kept on kissing her all the same, and she closed her eyes as his mouth travelled over her neck and his teeth nibbled erotically at the lobes of her ears. 'So this is what a witch tastes like—like cherries. Or strawberries or—'

'Or plums?'

'Hmm.' Then he spluttered as he burrowed into her hair and she came back with a little jolt.

'Hair gel,' she gurgled, and began to laugh softly, stretching out to run her finger across his jaw. 'It's stuck to your chin.'

'All the more wizardly to eat you with,' he growled, and pulled her against him again. But she shook her head, half laughing still.

'No, we can't, Daniel.'

'Wizards can,' he growled, refusing to release her. 'That's the fun of being able to do magic.'

Then something crashed in the hall and the door flew open. They sprang apart just in time as two little boys burst in with bright painted faces and long green hair. Helen followed with a tray of empty dishes in her arms.

'A wizard's here!' one of them shrieked, jumping up and down. 'Are you really a wizard?'

Daniel nodded convincingly. 'Of course I am.'

'Are you nice or nasty?'

'Nice—most of the time.' Then he crouched and growled and sprang at them, and they ran out screaming.

Helen burst into laughter. 'You look wonderful, Daniel! How long have you been here?'

'Just arrived,' Daniel said, and glanced quickly at Alex, who managed to hide a blush. She didn't think her mother had guessed what had gone on, and even if she had she was tactful enough to ignore it as she laid the tray on the table and opened the kitchen door. Daniel stepped cautiously into the hall and was instantly drowned by the delighted shrieks of eight ebullient children.

Grant Durrant arrived a few minutes after eight. Emma gave Alex and Helen a hug and giggled at a disrobed Daniel, who dug into the sack and produced a rubbery snake.

'It's a bit like the one we found that day,' she said, and her eyes lit up as Alex helped her on with her coat. 'In my aunty June's garden.'

Daniel grinned. 'But you'll be able to keep this one under your pillow.'

Emma looked up at her father. 'Can I, Daddy?'

'Of course you can, sweetheart.'

'For always?'

Grant looked slightly confused at Emma's persistence, and then nodded. 'We'd better go. Have you said thank you to Dr Trent?'

'Thank you for a nice party,' Emma murmured, and coiled the snake into her pocket. 'Bye, Cossie.'

'Bye, Emma. See you.'

The tall, slim man smiled and led his daughter out, and Helen and Alex busied themselves with seeing off the rest of the children.

When all the children had gone, and Daniel had disposed of the rubbish, Alex sent Cosmo upstairs to get ready for bed. 'Let's spoil ourselves with a treat,' Helen suggested, and carved three slices of chocolate gateau and made hot, strong coffee, setting it all on a tray. After Cosmo had tucked down, Helen took the tray in beside the fire.

'Worth wizarding for,' Daniel praised, and demolished his.

Helen laughed. 'There's more, if you'd like it.'

'Don't tempt me.' He glanced at Alex, who sat beside him on the sofa. 'Was Emma all right?' he asked curiously.

Alex slid her plate onto the coffee table and sighed. 'No, actually. She's fretting she won't be able to stay with her father again.'

'But why?' Daniel frowned.

'Because of the baby. She thinks there won't be room for her.'

'But that's not true, is it?'

Alex shrugged. 'I shouldn't think so. To be honest, I don't know where he's living. But wherever it is I'm sure he wouldn't have said that to Emma. She's just drawn the conclusion that she won't be wanted.'

'Which is probably why she's been unhappy,' Helen remarked softly. 'I met June in Tyllington the other day and she told me that Ollie's very worried about her.'

Alex nodded. 'Ollie doesn't say much, but it must be awful for her.'

'Does she know Emma feels this way?' Daniel asked, his face concerned.

'I've no idea,' Alex replied, and laid her head back on the sofa. 'And I don't know whether I should bring it up.'

'But surely you must,' Helen said in surprise.

'I could do more harm than good, Mum,' Alex answered doubtfully. 'What if I caused a further rift between Grant and Ollie by repeating what Emma told me? Ollie might believe that Grant is really ignoring her—or, worse, abandoning their daughter in favour of the baby.'

'Tricky.' Daniel nodded.

'Poor Emma,' Helen sighed. 'She was such a little extrovert once.'

A silence descended and they each sat with their thoughts.

Alex never failed to think how fortunate she was with Cosmo and the way he seemed to accept Zak's flying visits. But then he had grown up with his father's colourful, if unconventional behaviour, and expected no more.

As for her own relationship with Zak... Well, there was friendship and a kind of loving. For Cosmo's sake they remained in touch, and Helen was always happy to have Zak to stay. But Zak's inconsistency worried her, and she feared that his interest in time might wane.

'Past my bedtime,' Helen said after a while, and smothered a yawn. She kissed Daniel on the cheek and then Alex. 'It was a lovely evening,' she said, and waggled a finger at Daniel. 'You missed your vocation, young man.'

'She's right,' Alex said when they were alone. 'Have you ever thought of taking up wizarding professionally?'

'Hmm,' he nodded, and bent to lift her shoeless feet onto his lap. 'I gave it some thought but decided the hours are a bit late. I'm more a daytime man myself. Though, I have to say wizarding has it compensations.' He slid her a mischievous glance and her cheeks crimsoned.

'Thank you for making the day special,' she said quietly.

'Did I?' Two dark eyebrows rose innocently.

'You know you did. The children loved it.' Alex tried to ignore the smooth, sensational touch of his fingers massaging her toes. But it seemed to be interfering with her train of thought so she dropped her head back on the cushions and grinned. 'I had an idea you might prove useful.'

'I see...' He pulled her down by her ankles and she screeched.

'Shh, you'll wake everyone,' he warned her as his fingers burrowed around her waist, and she had to smother her laughter.

'Stop tickling me, Daniel. I'm hopeless!'

She rolled into a ball but he kept tickling her, and suddenly they were laughing so much that her eyes were filled with happy tears. Daniel brought her against him in a huge bear hug and she lifted her face, trying to catch her breath.

Then quite suddenly they were still. He held her against him and her heart looped the loop as she gazed into his eyes, so beautifully silver. It was all she could do to breathe.

'This is where we left off, little witch.' He breathed on her face and twirled one of her green spikes behind her ear. 'And it's oh, so tempting to continue.'

'Daniel…'

'I know. Don't say it.'

'It's been so good.'

'It's always good with us—or haven't you noticed?' he asked her gently as she lay curled in his arms.

She hadn't consciously. She hadn't wanted to. And now, as she thought how perfect it was, she just couldn't bear the truth. Don't let me fall in love with him again, she pleaded silently. Please don't. He's going away and I have a life to lead—and there's Cossie to think of…

And the reasons went rolling around in her head like rocks from an avalanche, tumbling down and causing havoc, enough of a warning for any sane person. But she wasn't sane when he held her like this, or touched her, or kissed her.

Then she looked into his eyes again and she saw a hunger there that matched her own. And nothing could take that away. No logic, no reason, no sensible distancing. There was hunger, raw and craving, and she wanted him so much.

'Alex…' His voice was rough as he brought his mouth down over her lips. It wasn't easy fun or gentle teasing any more. It was much more than that. Oh, so much more. And she clung to him, opening her mouth and letting all the goodness in, her hands drawing him to her with desperation.

There's nothing more I want, she thought crazily as he kissed her. I just want this, to be here, in his arms and kissing him. Nothing mattered, just the moment and their crazy need. Then his hand slid over her breast and she arched and gave a little cry. And that only seemed to make things worse as he dragged her closer and his kiss became deep and urgent. His fingers caressed the tiny buds and they traitorously peaked.

Wanting his touch to go on for ever, she felt his arousal was almost more than she could bear. She was so close to doing something she'd regret. And regret it she would. They had no future, he'd made no promises, and yet…

Then there was a little click and a shuffle, and Daniel moved slightly. Alex heard it too and sat up, glancing quickly over the sofa. 'Cossie?'

A little figure shuffled in. Daniel jumped up, hurried over and hunkered down. 'Hi, tiger. Couldn't you sleep?'

'I had a dream and woke up.'

Daniel threaded an arm around the small shoulders. 'What sort of dream?'

'I was with Nanna and Pops and we were at the zoo.'

'Sounds good to me.' Daniel smiled.

'But we couldn't find Daddy.'

'Maybe he was looking at the animals.'

Cosmo gave a little nod and Daniel lifted him up and brought him to the sofa. 'Cuddle up with Mummy and I'll get you a drink.'

Alex looked up gratefully as Cosmo snuggled against her. 'Cold milk, please, Daniel. There's plenty in the fridge.'

She wrapped her arms around the lean little body clad in pyjamas and inhaled the sleepy aroma—a scent midway between babyhood and growing up, with a tinge of freshly laundered cotton.

'I like Daniel being here,' he said sleepily as she stroked the damp hair from his forehead. 'Why can't he come back to stay with us?'

'Because he's only in England for a while, darling.'

'When is he going away?'

'After Christmas,' Alex said gently.

'Is that when we're going to leave Grandma's and go back to our old house?'

'No, it won't be quite so soon.'

'I wish we could stay here for ever,' the wispy voice murmured sleepily, 'and that Daniel wasn't going away.'

Alex bit her lip. She hadn't wanted this—not Cossie's little heart broken. She knew that whatever she said to ease the absence of Daniel it wouldn't help. You and me both, darling child, she thought, and the question of their future loomed uneasily in her mind. Yes, she'd be able to return to hospital life as she'd planned, to buy a flat, to start all over again. But her enthusiasm wasn't there and somehow she had to recover it.

A few minutes later Daniel appeared with the milk and she eased herself up from the cushions.

'Too late,' he mouthed, smiling down at Cosmo, and he put the milk aside.

'It was just a dream,' she whispered. 'I'll take him up to bed.'

'Let me,' Daniel insisted, and bent to lift him, wedging him firmly against his chest and treading carefully across the floor. Alex led the way and smoothed the ruffled bed, then together they covered him and turned off the night light.

Downstairs, Daniel took hold of her arm, pulled her against him and held her close. 'I must go now,' he told her in low voice.

She ached for him to stay. But he kissed her gently, gathered his coat and whispered that he would see her on Monday. She let him into the back garden and watched his tall form slip silently down the path to the gate and disappear through it into the forest.

Quietly she came back in and sat on the sofa, running her hand over the dimpled cushions. If she could only stop wanting him. If she could instruct her weak body not to ache so much. If only she had a little self-control.

'Some hopes,' she whispered, and squirmed into the warm

hollow of Daniel's shape for comfort. Which was where she fell asleep, inhaling his aroma on the linen as even her dreams allowed her no peace.

November brought coughs and colds and the usual array of winter ills. By November the fifth most of the flu jabs had been given, but one or two stragglers drifted in, and Alex was in the small treatment room when Daniel appeared. He poked his head round the open door and raised an eyebrow.

'More jabs?'

'No, all done.' She smiled. 'I'm waiting for someone rather elderly and Sue had to see her to the loo. The poor woman's ears were dreadful—stuffed with wax. I want to check them out just to be sure.'

He nodded, then came in and gestured to the window. 'I've spotted a few fireworks already.' He turned to her. 'Are you doing anything with Cossie tonight?'

'Nothing planned.' She shrugged. 'Are you still taking him to the bonfire on Saturday?'

'If Cossie would like to, then yes.' Just then Sue's voice echoed along the corridor and Daniel stepped back, opening the door as he did so. 'Starts at seven. Come too, if you like.'

She wanted to, but she'd spent the past days lecturing herself and attempting to be strong. And what was the use of all that if she caved in at the first hurdle?

'Thanks, but no—' she began as Sue appeared with Mrs Jeeves on her arm.

'Hello, Mrs Jeeves.' Alex smiled at the eighty-two-year-old lady who made her way carefully in.

'Hello, Dr Trent. I can hear very well now, thank you—now that the nurse has seen to them.'

'Good. Come and sit down and we'll just make certain about that little bit of earache, though I'm sure you're just fine.'

'Must fly,' Sue Peach said, relinquishing her charge. 'My next patient's in.'

'Me too.' Daniel nodded. 'So we'll leave it at that, then?'

Alex nodded and met his eyes briefly. Then he was gone and Mrs Jeeves was settling herself in the chair.

'How wonderful to find all you young things so busy,' she said brightly. 'It reminds me of my father's practice. Wonderful days. I loved all his patients. I hated to see them go— some of them were adorable.'

'Your father was a doctor?' Alex asked in surprise.

'No, a veterinary, my dear.'

'Oh, I see.' Alex laughed as she examined her patient's right ear. 'You were talking about the animals.'

'Indeed. It was wonderful for my brother and I, but my mother had a time of it. We lived in the Midlands, in farming country. It was strange how calves were always born during the middle of the night.'

'She must have been a very tolerant woman,' Alex observed with a smile.

'In fact, she was the reverse,' Mrs Jeeves admitted, and chuckled. 'But the animals always came first, and when my brother qualified as a veterinary and went into partnership with my father her temper didn't improve. She used to say that having one vet in the family was enough, but two was madness. So of course, although I wanted to be a vet too, it was completely out of the question.'

'That's such a shame.' Alex sat down and sighed wistfully. 'I was lucky. My father was a surgeon and both my parents encouraged me.'

'Then you've been blessed,' Mrs Jeeves pronounced. 'And is that your young man who just left?'

'Dr Hayward?' Alex said, slightly startled. 'What makes you say that?'

Mrs Jeeves raised her eyebrows. 'My dear, I may be old, and a little deaf, but I can still recognise an adoring male when I see one.' Alex felt her cheeks flame and Mrs Jeeves smiled. 'I'm sorry if I've embarrassed you.'

'No, you haven't, but—' Alex said flusteredly, and was silenced by a firmly raised palm.

'Not another word. It'll be our little secret!'

Alex looked into her patient's astute gaze and swallowed. 'Better get you done,' she said quickly, and completed the rest of her examination with some difficulty as Mrs Jeeves warmed to her theme.

By the time she helped the elderly lady to her waiting taxi Alex found herself smiling. Human nature was surprising— never more so if you judged by appearances. The prim-looking little lady had survived three husbands and as many lovers, and wasn't finished yet. Her neighbour had lost his wife and was in need of comfort.

'I would rather be sorry for something I've done,' she had said as she left, 'than for something that I didn't do.'

Me too, Alex thought as she returned to surgery. Only I'm not so brave.

CHAPTER NINE

COSSIE was excited all day, and had his coat on long before Daniel arrived. Minutes later they were driving off, and Alex tried to ignore the pang of regret that she wasn't going with them. Her mother had gone out and she wasn't on call. She had time to herself for once.

Not that she had planned much. In fact she was definitely at a loose end. Her attempt to watch a movie on the television was futile. You wanted to go with them, a little voice kept saying. And finally, irritated beyond words with her inability to concentrate, she hauled Suzie out for a walk.

By the time she arrived back it was half past nine. Daniel had said the bonfire would be over at ten, so she put on fresh coffee and heated croissants, and glanced several times at the clock over the fire.

When ten o'clock passed she went to the window and glanced out. Her heart jiggled at the sight of the figure approaching the front door. Then she realised it was Helen, and her friend Jean was just driving off.

'Not home yet?' Helen bustled in, her cheeks bright pink from the cold. She took off her coat and scarf and looked expectantly from the little porch window.

'No—perhaps the bonfire went on longer.'

'You should have gone, darling.'

'Mum—'

'I know.' Helen turned and smiled. 'So, what have you been up to?'

'Oh, this and that.' Alex looked away. 'Did you have a good evening?'

'Better than yours, I would imagine.' Helen chuckled as she linked her arm through her daughter's. 'We had our usual

116

chat and a glass of wine. Well, at least I did. Jean was driving. Oh, I think I just heard a car door.'

They doubled back to the window and Alex smiled. 'Yes, there's Cossie.'

'Mum, look what I've got,' he said breathlessly, tugging off his hat and scarf. 'Sparklers. You can light them indoors. They're special ones.'

'But probably the garden would be better,' Daniel said as he came in, grinning. 'And probably not tonight. It's late— I'm sorry. We lost track of time.'

'Was it a good bonfire?' Alex thought how the cold weather suited him, his face glowing with good health and his eyes sparkling like bright silver stars. Then she noticed how well Cossie looked too, his pale complexion flushed with fresh air and his eyes bright with excitement. She found herself thinking how Cossie never looked like that with Zak. Then felt so bad for thinking it that she completely forgot to offer a warm drink as Daniel hovered on the doorstep.

'Daniel, you will stay, won't you?' Helen asked politely. 'Warm yourself up with something hot to eat?'

Daniel slid a glance at Alex. 'Thanks, Helen, but I won't. Though I'm sure Cossie will.'

'Thank you for taking me to the bonfire,' Cossie said, without prompting.

Daniel hunkered down and aimed a teasing punch to his shoulder. 'You're welcome, tiger. Sleep well.'

Cosmo giggled and almost hugged him, but scuttled off instead.

'Goodnight, Daniel.' Helen smiled and followed her grandson.

'Thank you,' Alex said as they stood alone, and Daniel shrugged.

'I had every excuse to have fun.' He gave her a twisted little grin. 'Ridiculous, isn't it? I really enjoyed tonight. It would have been nice if you'd come, though.'

And because she couldn't bear having to resist wrapping

her arms around him and saying she wished she had gone too, she mumbled a pathetic excuse.

'Well, I'll let you get on,' he said gruffly, and opened the door. 'Goodnight, Alex.'

She felt crushed when he'd gone. Which is exactly what you deserve, Alex Trent, she told herself as she turned to the kitchen. You left Mum to ask him in whilst you stood there like a prune. And you couldn't even think of a reasonable excuse for not going.

Her mood wasn't helped as she walked in and saw her mother opening the oven.

'Well, this is a challenge,' Helen sighed as she lowered the steaming croissants to the table. 'We'll have to eat them all ourselves.'

'I can eat two.' Cosmo scooped up a chair and licked his lips. 'I said to Daniel that you'd probably make us supper.'

'And what did he say?' Helen asked as she sat beside him.

'That he was famished.'

'Then he should have stayed,' Alex said indignantly.

A remark that caused Helen to look up with raised eyebrows.

For some time afterwards, Daniel seemed to be doing all he could to avoid her. Not that his attitude had changed. He was still pleasant, and spoke to her when they met. But there was definitely a distancing between them.

Well, you've got what you wanted, haven't you? she kept telling herself. Then the next moment was missing him so much that she almost—almost—found ways to bump into him. But she didn't descend to quite that level, because she knew she couldn't live with herself if she did.

Ramming home the facts every so often helped. Daniel was a temporary aberration, a sweet torture that she had to endure until either he left the practice or she did. Plain and simple. They would be going their own ways and this mad interlude would be over. Done with. Finished. And the less she got involved the better. She had fallen into that trap with him years ago, and she couldn't risk it again. That was the truth and she tried to remind herself of it daily.

But one Sunday afternoon, towards the end of November, the phone rang and it was Daniel. 'Alex—I'm at Marl Wood,' he told her urgently. 'I'm with Stephen Hurd. He's your patient, isn't he?'

'Stephen—yes—what's wrong?'

'He's sick, very feverish, and making no sense.'

'You're in Marl Wood?'

'Yes, by the car park. Can you come?'

'Cossie's out for tea, but my mother will be here by the time he gets back. I'll be there in ten minutes.'

She pulled on some jeans and threw on a sweater and jacket. When Helen arrived back with Suzie, she said she would be there for Cossie, and within a few minutes Alex found herself in the car heading towards Marl, wondering how on earth both Daniel and Stephen had got there.

By the time she arrived the sun had slipped below the trees, and she only just missed the rabbits that shot across her path. The car park was deserted, except for Daniel's blue car. The wood was much darker than she'd expected. She climbed out and locked her car, then looked both ways, but nothing moved. Then she heard gravel crunching and saw the outline of a tall figure striding towards her.

'It's me, Alex,' Daniel said hurriedly, and she knew by the tone of his voice something was wrong. 'I'm sorry to bring you out,' he apologised as he reached and took her arm. 'I'll leave all explanations until later, if you don't mind. But for now I was hoping you'd be able to persuade Stephen to come in my car. I want to take him to the hospital.'

'The hospital?' she mumbled as they hurried towards the wood. 'He's that sick?'

'Oh, yes, he's sick all right.' Just then they heard a voice, and Alex saw someone stumbling around in the fern.

'Heavens, Stephen, what are you doing here?' she gasped as they neared.

'Try…trying to find my pigs,' he gulped, and wiped sweat from his forehead with the back of his sleeve.

'Lord knows how long he's been here,' Daniel whispered as Stephen wandered round aimlessly, kicking the under-growth and stumbling.

'Stephen—I'd like you to go with Dr Hayward,' Alex called calmly. 'You're in no fit state to wander around like this.'

'No way. You're not going to touch me,' Stephen mut-tered, and sank against a tree. Alex could see that it was all he could do to stand up.

'Come on, Stephen,' Alex coaxed gently. 'It's dark any-way. You won't be able to see a thing soon.'

'I'll go…when…when I find her—my sow,' he rasped, his breath coming in wheezy gasps. 'She—she's been lost for two days.'

'But this is the forest,' Daniel protested. 'She could be anywhere.'

'No, she likes it here. She likes the fern. I…I come here to cut it for her…' The big man went to kick the bracken with a boot but his legs buckled. He swayed, grabbing at the tree, and sank to his knees. Daniel and Alex rushed forward and Daniel yanked an arm around his shoulders. He hiked Stephen to his feet and pulled him away from the tree. 'Do you think you can manage walking to the car?' Daniel asked, but got no response as Stephen's head lolled forward.

'He's burning up and delirious,' Alex sighed, and lifted his other arm and dragged it around her shoulders. Somehow they managed to haul him back through the woods and finally into the car park. Daniel unlocked his car and dropped him carefully in.

'Can you get hold of a relative?' he asked as he folded Stephen's legs under the dashboard. 'I need to ask a few questions.'

'His girlfriend, Gail, lives at the cottage.' Alex nodded.

'That'll do. Try to find her and bring her to the hospital.'
Alex nodded, though she was still puzzled. 'I'll try.'

'When I see you I'll explain everything,' Daniel promised as he hurried round to the other side and gazed across the roof. It was so dark that she could barely see his features. 'Thanks for coming, Alex.'

Then he disappeared and the engine started up with a roar. In seconds his car was heading northwards and Alex waited, watching the tail-lights fade. Then she climbed into her car and headed after them, wondering what she would do if she couldn't find Gail.

She needn't have worried. Gail was in the yard and the animals were in shelter for the night. The five-bar gate was closed, but there was a light on in the old barn at the back and Alex trudged round there. Gail was unloading bales from a truck, and when she saw Alex she dropped the hay and came running over.

'It's Stephen, isn't it?' she asked in a hoarse whisper. 'Something's happened.'

'Dr Hayward's with him. He's taken him to hospital—'

'Dr Hayward?' Gail interrupted. 'But how…? Why…?'

'I don't know.' Alex shrugged, beginning to shiver in the cold air. 'He found Stephen in Marl Wood and he looked sick. So he's taken him in.'

Gail closed her eyes and leaned against the door of the barn. Her breath curled up into the air. Frost had begun to silver the wood behind her head. 'I knew it,' she breathed, shaking her head slowly. 'I knew he was ill and he kept saying he was all right.'

'When did he say he was ill?' Alex asked.

'Oh…I don't know,' Gail muttered, and opened her eyes. 'Yesterday—the day before? He was hot and irritable and I thought he might have flu.'

'Didn't you think it might be the original problem again?'

Gail lifted her shoulders in a shrug. 'I didn't want to think about it. You just don't stand a chance with Stephen. He could be the living dead and still the animals would come first. I honestly don't know why I put up with it.'

'Because you love him?' Alex offered simply.

Gail nodded slowly. 'Look, I'll get some other clothes on. I can't go in these.' She gestured to her filthy jodhpurs and boots.

Inside the cottage it was warm and a log fire was burning. Alex warmed her hands whilst Gail went to change. 'Tell me what happened,' Gail shouted from the bedroom.

'I had a call from Dr Hayward to tell me that he'd found Stephen at Marl, wandering around.'

'I didn't want him to go out,' yelled Gail. 'But he's lost Dinni, his sow. She's been gone a couple of days. He went on foot too. Said he had a better chance of finding her.'

'Would he really take so much trouble over one pig?' Alex asked incredulously.

'Over a pig, yes,' came the swift reply. 'Or a pony. As for me…'

There was silence then, until Gail returned wearing clean cords and a jumper. Her auburn hair was tied back in a ponytail and she was carrying a book in her hands. 'Here you are,' she said, thrusting it at Alex. 'The precious diary. Though what you'll find in it beats me. One-liners, most of it.'

'Where did you find it?' Alex asked, and tucked it into her pocket.

'Where I find most of Stephen's treasures.' Gail hiked a wax jacket from a peg by the door. 'In the barn, under a bale of hay.' She gave a short laugh. 'He must have written in it whilst he was out there. Which isn't really surprising. That's where he spends most of his life.'

They were just about to leave when the telephone rang. Gail hurried to answer it. 'So what do you want us to do?'

she asked bleakly. Then she nodded, replaced the receiver and glanced at Alex. 'That was Dr Hayward. It's pneumonia.'

Alex wasn't surprised and she looked at Gail. 'There's no point in going over tonight, is there?'

'No.' Gail sank into a chair. 'What will they do?'

'X-rays—find out all they can.' Alex shrugged. 'And then treat him.'

'With what?' Gail asked croakily.

Alex paused. 'Antibiotics or antifungals, and put him on ventilation if he's really struggling.'

'Is it something to do with his illness?' Gail asked after a pause.

'Possibly. Which is one good reason for having those tests. This might never have happened if he had.'

'Tell me about it,' Gail groaned. 'We've had the most unholy quarrels since then. He just won't listen to reason.'

'But surely he could find someone to care for his animals?' Alex asked in surprise.

'Oh, yes. He could if he tried.'

'So where's the problem, then?'

Gail's eyes suddenly went moist. 'I suppose I should have told you before, but Stephen made me promise not to. You see, Stephen once had an older brother. He was a farmer, very fit and able. In his mid-thirties—like Stephen—he got married, and two days after the wedding he collapsed and died. Apparently he had a dodgy heart and no one knew about it.'

Alex was shocked. 'Stephen's never mentioned it.'

'He wouldn't. He's too proud of his health and of being a Commoner. After his parents died he took the responsibility of this place and the animals all on his shoulders, certain he could cope. When Barry died it hit him really hard. You must have guessed by now that he thinks because he has this mystery complaint he has the same problem as Barry.'

'But I don't understand, Gail,' Alex said in dismay. 'The tests would have shown any indications of heart disease—'

'And then what?' Gail broke in. 'Take things easy? No heavy manual work? No intensive labour? No animals? Give up all that generations of Hurds have worked so hard to achieve?' She shook her head resolutely. 'Stephen would never come to terms with half-measures.'

'So he'd rather go on without treatment?' Alex said in exasperation.

'No...' Gail turned slowly and looked at her. 'He'd simply rather not go on. If he couldn't work he wouldn't want to—well, you know...' Her words faded and she looked away.

Alex heaved in a breath. 'Is this what you were going to tell me that night we looked for the diary?'

Gail nodded. 'I promised Stephen never to breathe a word.'

'But if you had I would have understood why Stephen acted the way he did at the hospital and I could have helped.'

'I'm sorry.' Gail slid her hand over a wet cheek.

'It's not your fault.' Alex sighed gently. 'He's lucky to have you.' She thought of all the things that had puzzled her and now made sense—Stephen's reluctance to admit to illness and his refusal to be treated by the hospital. Maybe he'd even lost the diary on purpose.

Gail shrugged. 'When you love someone you stand by them—whatever.'

Alex smiled. 'Stephen's a lucky man.'

'I just hope he can cope with what's ahead,' Gail murmured anxiously, and looked slowly up at Alex.

After calling Daniel to tell him about Stephen's brother's death from heart disease, Alex phoned her mother to let her know what had happened, and Helen said that she was in all evening and she needn't rush back. Cosmo spoke to her briefly and told her about his day with Marcus. The pang of guilt that she wasn't with him lingered unpleasantly. And it wasn't until she found Gail in the bedroom, in tears, that she completely forgot her own concerns.

Gail mopped her eyes and Alex made a hot cup of tea and sat with her.

'I'm two years older than Stephen,' she sniffed as they sat on the edge of the bed. 'Thirty-seven is late to start a family. And anyway I wouldn't, not if we didn't get married. It wouldn't be fair to the kids.'

'Some people don't bother,' Alex said hesitantly.

'Not me. I want my kids to have a name, an identity.' She stuffed her tissue into her sleeve and sipped her tea. 'I'm fostered, and I've always wondered…'

Alex watched her fight for words, then nodded. 'Who your parents were?'

'Yes.'

'How long have you and Stephen been together?'

'Eight years.' She laughed softly then. 'And likely to be together another eight before he pops the question.'

Alex stared into her tea and wondered what would have happened if she and Daniel had stuck it out. If she had lasted in the race against time and they'd married and started a family. Would she have accepted living together if he'd never proposed? Perhaps she had been too young to care then. She'd certainly felt he put his family before their relationship. And yet would time have resolved those issues too? Probably. After all, he'd been working abroad for years. So his parents must have coped in his absence. Funny, she hadn't thought of that before, and now it made her feel slightly weird. Maybe if she hadn't given him that ultimatum—maybe…

'Someone's coming,' Gail said, and jumped up. They hurried into the hallway just as the front door opened.

Daniel stood there, the collar of his heavy jacket pulled up. His dark hair fell in spikes over his forehead and he rubbed his hands, flexing his fingers.

'I waited until I knew a bit more,' he said, and looked at Gail. 'He's comfortable, and they've started him on antibiotics. When I left he didn't look half as bad as he did earlier.

Tomorrow there should be signs of improvement, but we'll just have to wait and see. Is there a hot drink going?'

Alex nodded. 'I've just made one.'

They sat in the kitchen and Alex poured tea. Gail produced some scones, fresh butter and some homemade jam, and then Alex showed Daniel the diary.

Daniel frowned as he looked at it. Then suddenly he jabbed the page with his finger. 'It's here!'

'What?' Alex and Gail spoke together.

'Look—this.' He drew his finger along two words.

Gail frowned. 'Forest—scything.' She looked bewilderedly at Daniel as he scooped the pages over.

'And here again—look, the same two words.'

'But what does it mean?' Alex asked.

'I'm willing to bet these entries match the dates that Stephen had his attacks. Or at least were *before* the attacks. There's one here, tenth of September, and another, second of October. And the latest—four days ago.'

'But how can scything have anything to do with his attacks?' Gail said incredulously. 'I mean, he does it all the time around this place. It's one of the things he boasts about—doing it the old-fashioned way, like his father and grandfather.'

'Gail—it's the word before that counts. Forest,' Daniel murmured.

'Why is scything in the forest any different to scything here?' Alex cut in.

'Throw on your coats and I'll show you,' Daniel said, and jumped up.

A few moments later they were standing outside the barn as Gail unlocked the big wooden doors. She flicked on the lights and a bird fluttered high in the roof. Their breath circled into the misty air and Alex pulled her jacket around her, grateful for its warmth.

'I still don't understand what we're doing here,' Gail said as Daniel moved amongst the bales of hay and animal food.

'We're looking for something,' Daniel replied, half hidden in the shadows. 'This wall here, Gail—it's wet.'

'Yes,' Gail said, and sighed. 'Stephen's been repairing it. The roof lets in the rain and water trickles down the side.'

'Is there an upstairs?'

'Yes, beside you—behind the pellet sacks.'

Daniel squeezed around the sacks and climbed them. Gail turned to Alex. 'There's nothing up there but some hay and a bit of bedding.'

'Up here!' Daniel called, and Gail hurried forward. Alex followed. Upstairs, under the eaves, Daniel was hunched in the corner. He was prodding a large polythene bag with his shoe and some of the contents spilled out onto the rafters.

A cloud of dust spread over them as he pulled out the bundle. 'Yuk,' Alex said, and coughed, fishing for a tissue. 'What is it?'

'It's not hay or straw.' Daniel unthreaded the string and opened the bundle. 'But it's mouldy and rotting, whatever it is.'

Gail bent down beside him and clasped a hand over her mouth. 'Heavens, that looks like bracken. Stephen's been clearing it out from the barn. He can't have found this up here. He got rid of most of it last week.'

'Does he always keep bracken in here?' Alex asked curiously.

'No, just this summer. He was short of space and needed to get it under cover. It was only a temporary arrangement until he got some extra storage space.'

'What does he use it for?'

'Well, bedding for the ponies occasionally, but mostly for Dinni, in her sty in the field. In the old days cutting the fern was a custom practised by the Commoners, but now it's swiped by machine. Although this year—'

'Stephen scythed it by hand,' Daniel ended, and Gail nodded.

'But what has the bracken got to do with Stephen's illness?'

'Everything,' Daniel said, heaving the bale back against the rafters. He stood up slowly and brushed down his jacket. 'I think Stephen suffers from something we call farmer's lung. It's a condition that develops after exposure to dust containing fungal spores. The organisms thrive in warm, damp conditions, and this barn's atmosphere is ideal—especially with that wet wall. You say Stephen's in here a lot, and moving this stuff around must have been lethal. It was inevitable that he inhaled the spores, and I think his pneumonia is a complication of the FL.'

'Of course,' Alex said in sudden understanding. 'The shortness of breath, the flu-like symptoms and the fever—'

'Is there a cure?' Gail interrupted, and Daniel raised his eyebrows slowly.

'It depends on whether the lungs have been damaged beyond repair, and we won't know that until the hospital is certain of what they're dealing with. Let's get out of here and into the cottage. I'll have to ring them and tell them what we've found.'

It was ten o'clock by the time they left Gail, and Alex drove home quickly, hoping Cossie might still be awake.

'Cossie's asleep,' Helen warned her when she arrived home. 'Come and have some soup. We'll sit by the fire.'

So they settled down and Alex explained the hunt they'd had in the barn.

'Poor Gail,' Helen sighed. 'But how clever of Daniel. What made him think of the bracken?'

'He said that it was whilst we were in Marl. Stephen insisted that his pig would be there, that she loved the fern he cut for her. The barn seemed the most likely place to store the stuff and Gail confirmed it. She said he'd got rid of most of it—presumably because it had gone off—but he'd missed the bit we found.'

'Are some people allergic to bracken?' Helen asked as they drank the hot soup. 'Doesn't Stephen deal with hay and straw all the time?'

'The bracken may have a type of allergic alveolitis, and Stephen could be hypersensitive to it,' Alex murmured thoughtfully. 'Anyway, the hospital will discover what's going on and we'll have to go from there.'

They sat in the glow of the fire and Alex wondered what Daniel was doing. She should have suggested he come back for some soup. After the hectic day it would have been good to sit with him and unwind.

What was he doing all alone in that big house? Was he sitting in one of those huge rooms that seemed so austere? Or was he showering, letting a flow of hot, soothing water relax his muscles? She shivered at the thought of the water cascading over his sleek, long body and then jerked up her head, glancing guiltily at Helen.

But she needn't have worried that her thoughts were readable. Helen was gazing into the fire. 'A penny for your thoughts, Mum,' she said, and Helen turned, her brow creased in a frown.

'I was wondering why Daniel was at Marl Wood today,' she said, and raised her eyebrows.

A question which had occurred to Alex too, but in the rush she'd forgotten to ask. Strange that he'd been there—had he seen Stephen from the road as he'd driven by? It seemed unlikely, since they'd been in the wood when she had arrived.

'I've no idea.' She shrugged and Helen nodded, hiding a smile.

CHAPTER TEN

Two days later, Gail phoned. 'Stephen's pumped full of antibiotics,' she told Alex worriedly.

'It's to be expected,' Alex sympathised. 'They'll crack it in the end.'

'We've been living under a shadow for so long.' Gail sighed. 'I don't know what to think.' She gave a brittle laugh. 'The funny thing is, I found Dinni. She was up at Marl and I coaxed her back to the cottage. I don't know why I bothered. She's the cause of all the trouble.'

'Or maybe not,' Alex murmured. 'At least now Stephen will have those tests.'

'Yes—you're right. He said last night that when—*if* he gets better, a lot's going to change and I want to believe him.'

Gail deserved better, Alex thought, but didn't say. There was a long way to go yet, and the biggest irony of all would be that Stephen's health fears about his heart might be confirmed.

Something happened at the beginning of December that Alex hadn't expected. Zak phoned her at work to say he was coming to England. She asked him when exactly and he said in a week or so—which, for Zak, was pretty specific.

She was trying not to feel irritable as she ended surgery and went out to Reception. Zak descended whenever he felt like it, and she wondered if he ever gave a thought to her life, her agenda. Not that she would object anyway, for Cossie's sake.

In Reception Ollie was on duty, and Alex noticed how thin and pale she was looking.

'How's Emma?' she asked, and Ollie shrugged.

'I'm worried about her, but what can I do? There's something wrong and she won't tell me.'

'Have you no idea what it could be?'

'I wish I had. And it's not as if I can speak to Grant about her. He's working all hours in his new job and hasn't been able to have Emma since Cosmo's party. She misses him terribly.'

'Maybe she just needs reassurance, Ollie.'

'Maybe. But she won't open up, Dr Trent, and you know what a livewire she was once.'

'Would she talk to me?' Alex asked hesitantly. 'Not here. Maybe at home?

Ollie looked brighter. 'She might.'

'We'll organise something, okay? Before Christmas.'

'Thanks.' Ollie nodded, then her gaze went over Alex's shoulder. 'Oh, Dr Hayward—do you want me to leave Monday completely clear?'

Alex turned as Daniel stood beside her and handed Ollie a small pile of records. 'Yes, you'd better, Ollie. If I'm back I'll help out with the evening calls.'

'Dr Barlow and Dr Ashley have surgeries until one. There's only a few calls so far, so it probably won't be necessary. Coffee before you go?'

'No thanks, Ollie. I want to get away before the roads get busy.'

'Where are you off to?' Alex asked in surprise.

'To London. Peter's on call and we don't seem rushed off our feet. I thought this would be a good time.'

'For what?' Alex swallowed on the blip in her chest.

'Didn't I say?' Daniel frowned. 'There's a chance of a project coming up in West Africa.' He said it so casually he might have been talking about the weather. 'A small research group interested in malnutrition. They're concentrating on related diseases: typhoid, shigellosis, cholera, amoebiasis, that sort of thing.'

'Research? But is that your field?' she asked stupidly.

'Not exactly. My interest will be on a more practical level, since I'm familiar with the area. The trip is funded by a large pharmaceutical conglomerate and could be interesting. Either that or a complete waste of time.' He shrugged lightly, as if to dismiss it, but she knew better.

She watched his face and knew that there was more. But he gave her no chance to ask as he added quickly, 'And what about you? Doing anything special?' He gave an easy, lop-sided little smile that made her wonder if she'd just imagined what he'd said.

'No—riding, possibly, with Cossie.' She looked into his eyes and tried to read his expression, but it was no good.

'Sounds fun. Behave yourself, though.' She smiled and nodded and stood waiting for more. Then he picked up his case and flicked a glance at the girls. 'See you Tuesday, if not before.'

'Okay, Dr Hayward.'

'Drive carefully,' Alex gulped, and quickly cleared her throat.

'You bet.' He turned then, his tall frame weaving its way through the trickle of patients coming in, and Alex was left with an awful gnawing inside. He'd said it as if it didn't really matter, wasn't important. But for heaven's sake—West Africa!

Somehow she struggled through her afternoon surgery. When she got home that night, she told her mother that Zak had rung.

'Where is he now?' Helen asked, almost amused.

'Italy, I think. Promoting some pop concert or other. He'll be seeing his parents some time in the next couple of weeks and he wants to know if he can stay.' Alex slid off her shoes and opened the fridge. She looked into it, seeing nothing.

Helen stopped what she was doing at the sink. 'What's wrong, darling?'

It's Daniel, she wanted to cry out. He's going away and

I'm not ready for it. And for all that I've said and done I haven't been able to stop loving him. Oh, Mum, I love him so much.

But instead she murmured, 'Nothing. I just wonder what Zak would do if I said it wasn't convenient.'

'Do you want to say that?'

'No. But Zak expects everything and gives nothing.'

'Well, Zak is—Zak,' Helen said, gently reproving. 'He's also Cossie's father. And you have to make allowances.' A little sigh passed through her lips. 'And, of course, he's not Daniel.'

And before Alex could reply she flicked on the food mixer.

Alex tried not to wish the weekend away. She'd missed riding so much, and this would be her first real opportunity for weeks.

It was beautiful weather, and she was given a sweet-tempered chestnut that knew the path well. Cossie's little roan trotted steadily in front and he bristled with pride. The forest track was dotted with heather and the sun was a soft December pink. There was no ice or frost and it was heaven in the fresh air.

Then suddenly the sky darkened and rain fell lightly. By half past four they were back at the stables and taking off the wet tack.

'I'm hungry,' Cossie complained as they left. 'What's for supper?'

'We'll celebrate Christmas early and eat out,' Alex decided as they got in the car. 'If Grandma's at home we'll ask her to come too.'

'Yummy.' Cossie giggled. 'Can we have pasta?'

'If you like.' Alex laughed. 'We'll try the little Italian in Tyllington.'

It was a delicious meal and should have been fun, and it was—mostly. But Alex still couldn't stop thinking about Daniel.

After the meal they abandoned the car and strolled through Tyllington. The shops were ablaze with Christmas lights and they stopped and gazed in. When it began to rain again Cossie insisted it was snow, so they went home laughing and singing carols full of seasonal cheer.

'We'll go out early to the forest tomorrow,' Helen suggested before bed. 'And choose a tree.'

'A big one,' Cossie yawned. 'Right up to the ceiling.'

'I'll put up some decorations tonight,' Alex told Helen after Cossie had gone to bed. 'I'm in the mood.'

She wasn't really. But it was better to pretend she was, rather than lie awake and go stir crazy thinking of Daniel.

'Can Emma come?' Cosmo asked at breakfast the next morning. 'To help put up the tree?'

'Good idea,' Helen said, and glanced at Alex.

'Can I phone her?' Cossie asked.

'All right, but she might not want to—or she might be busy.'

'She's not,' Cossie said as he jumped up. 'She told me at school.'

Alex frowned. 'What did she say?'

'Just that she was going to her dad's, but she isn't now.'

'Well,' said Helen after a pause, 'I'll make a sponge and a fruit cake. And if Emma comes we can toast some crumpets by the fire.'

Cossie went to ring Emma and came running back. 'Emma's mum wants to speak to you,' he told Alex.

Alex piled the dishes on the worktop and went to the phone. 'Hi, Ollie. Is it all right for Emma to come today?'

'Yes. Perfect. I was wondering what we could do on our own. Grant was supposed to be taking her to see Father Christmas, but he's got this new job and he's working. Shall I drive her over?'

'No, we'll collect her on our way to buy the tree.' When Alex rang off, she wondered if today she might be able to talk to Emma. But it would be difficult—unless the child spoke up voluntarily.

'Can she come?' Cossie asked eagerly in the kitchen.

'Yes. We'll collect her on our way to buy the tree.'

'Can we sing carols—and can we—?'

Alex smiled and drew his soft head against her. 'Whoa, there! It's not Christmas yet.'

'Even Daniel might come today. He did at Hallowe'en. I knew he was the wizard, really.'

A remark that had Alex laughing and sighing at the same time. Despite the impact that Daniel had made on Cossie's life he was miles away, and probably hadn't given them a thought. A sad fact of life, but she must come to terms with it. And eventually Cossie would too.

'Can I put up the star?' Emma asked as they packed away the boxes that had been filled with decorations. The tree looked stunning. Little lights twinkled and fingers of tinsel ran through the green branches. All that was left was the star Emma had been clutching for the last ten minutes.

'Careful climbing the ladder,' Alex warned. 'Go slowly. I'll be behind you.'

Emma started to climb. 'Mummy's only got a pretend tree.'

'Lovely.' Helen smiled as she held the stepladder. 'You'll have just as much fun.'

'Jesus didn't even have a bed,' Cossie piped up. 'He didn't even have any clothes.'

Alex hid her smile. 'Lean over a little, Emma, and clip the star to the top.'

'Like this?'

'Wonderful.'

When they came down Helen applauded. 'Well done, Emma.'

Afterwards they sat in the conservatory and ate Helen's cake. Then Cossie helped Helen clear away while Emma and

Alex put on their coats and took Suzie in the garden. 'I wish I had a dog,' Emma said. 'My daddy has.'

'What's his name?' Alex asked.

'Spot, 'cos he's got spots. I'd like to have a dog. But Mummy said they need a lot of looking after.' Emma trapped her lip. 'Like babies.'

'Yes, but babies grow up,' Alex pointed out. 'Then you'll be able to play with your baby brother or sister and have fun.'

Emma shook her head slowly. 'But I won't.'

'Why do you say that, Emma?'

'Because…because…I heard Daddy saying to Mummy that there won't be enough room for me to stay any more.'

Alex squeezed her hand. 'If I were you I would ask Mummy about what you heard.'

'She'll be cross. She says I mustn't listen to grown-ups' conversations.'

'You weren't listening.' Alex shrugged. 'You just happened to overhear something that is very important to you. And if you tell Mummy that she'll understand.'

'Will she?'

Alex nodded. 'Promise.'

Emma seemed brighter after that, and they brought Daniel's sparklers onto the lawn and lit them. Emma and Cossie held them at arm's length and made steamy vapour trails.

'Hi!' a voice called, and Alex turned to see a small figure in boots and a coat walking round the side of the house.

'Hi, Ollie, just in time for our finale.'

Emma came running up then. 'Mummy, look at me!' She danced round the lawn with her sparkler and they all laughed.

'That's more like her old self,' Ollie said as they watched the children. 'What if Cossie came back with us for a sleepover? I'll run them in to school in the morning.'

'Are you sure?' Alex asked.

'Perfectly. It'll be company for Emma.'

'Ollie, Emma spoke to me today,' Alex said quickly. And she told her what Emma had said.

'But she must have only heard half of our conversation,' Ollie gasped. 'You see, Grant's moving house soon. It's bigger, and Emma will be able to stay there. As I told you, her dad has got this new executive job. Even the girl he's with is complaining he's not home enough.' Ollie's eyebrows went up. 'Well, with two families to support it's not surprising, is it?'

'Ah.' Alex nodded. 'And Emma translates that into not being wanted.'

'Poor little love,' Ollie sighed. 'If only I'd known what was going on in her head. I've kept things back, not wanting to hurt her. Obviously I need to explain.'

Later Alex packed Cossie's rucksack and gave Ollie his school lunchbox. The two children ran excitedly to Ollie's car and Alex waved them off.

Helen was on the phone when she got back in. 'That was Jean,' she said, and glanced at her watch. 'She's coming to collect me in half an hour. We're going to see a movie. Come with us, if you like.'

'Thanks, Mum, maybe next time.'

'You don't know what you're missing,' Helen chuckled, and went off to get ready.

Alex strung a few more decorations on the tree until Jean called and whisked Helen off. Then Alex found herself wandering aimlessly around the house, trying hard not to think of Daniel.

The doorbell rang.

Assuming Helen had forgotten her key, she hurried to answer it. But the figure that stood there was tall and broad-shouldered, and for a moment she blinked, unable to believe her eyes.

'Hello,' Daniel said huskily. 'This is probably not a good time.'

'It's a very good time,' she said, and threw her arms

around him, burying her face in his coat. He smelt wonderfully of cold night air, and inhaling him made her feel weak with joy.

'Wow.' Daniel half laughed as he hugged her. 'I didn't expect this.'

'Nor did I,' she sniffed. 'I thought you'd be miles away by now.'

'I was, but then I had this irresistible urge to drive home.' He held her at arm's length and stared at her, then shunted the door closed with his heel and tipped up her chin. 'I missed you, Alex.'

'And I missed you.'

He bent to kiss her, teasing her lips with little flicks of his tongue, softly at first. Then she found herself clinging to him and there was no hesitation. In the glow of the Christmas tree he held her so tightly she thought he would never let her go.

When he did, he asked tautly, 'Are you alone?'

She nodded. 'Everyone's out.'

His eyes told her exactly what he wanted, what they both needed so desperately. And she took his hand and led him upstairs.

It had been a long, long time. Almost a decade too long.

Alex knew that whatever happened tomorrow she couldn't stop what was happening tonight. She wanted him more than she wanted anything. And she knew that he wanted her too.

She had imagined his hands undressing her, touching her, arousing her. She'd lain awake and imagined slowly undressing him. But even before they reached the bed he'd torn off his coat and shirt and dispensed with her blouse and jeans.

They lay adrift on the floor, the light blue of her silk blouse catching the bedside light, her jeans strewn somewhere in a heap. His mouth found hers with a frightening need as they fell onto the cool sheets and his fingers skilfully found the clip of her bra.

Then he looked at her as they lay there, her body under

his, and he brushed back her hair over the pillow. 'I want you so much, Alex. I couldn't stay away. I had to come back.'

She held his face between her hands. 'Daniel, hold me.'

There was no need for words as he slid off her bra and kissed the swell of her breasts. Her nipples pressed urgently against his mouth and he did something unimaginable with his tongue, sending an aching groan from her throat.

'Oh, Alex,' he muttered, and slid against her, and she responded to the subtle rhythm of his stroking and teasing. She arched, closing her eyes as he thrust his tongue again and again between her parted lips.

Her bra and panties joined the heap on the floor and soon all was lost, past and present colliding in breathless wonder.

When her fingers found the place on his chest that was cropped and roughened with short black hair, she froze. 'Your wound,' she whispered. 'I forgot. Did I hurt you?'

In response he lifted her hand and kissed it, then placed it back on his chest. 'You heal me,' he told her, and her face crumpled.

'Oh, Daniel, I wish I could have.'

'Nothing's changed,' he murmured against her ear. 'You're still as beautiful, womanly and sexy, and all the other things I remember. And wanted and needed so much.' He wrapped her tightly against him, as if shutting out the past, yet knowing he couldn't.

Moments passed, then he found her gaze and slid a finger along the line of her mouth. 'Oh, Alex, we've wasted so much time.'

She wanted to say that she thought that too. She wanted to hold him closer, slip into his skin if she could. She wanted to be part of him, to make up for the mistakes and give them a future…

Then she stiffened, knowing there couldn't be a future, and for a moment everything fell back into place. He seemed to sense it as he touched her, frowning a little, then smoothing his hand over her cheeks and into her hair.

'Come back here,' he growled. 'This is for us. For now.'

Tension built as he caressed her and little moans escaped from her lips. He explored her tenderly, her hips lifting as he moved with her, his mouth drifting agonisingly slowly over her body. She needed little coaxing as he slipped between her legs. He didn't hurt her, and she would hardly have known if he had. She was in another world, somewhere far beyond reality.

His kisses burnt her lips. His tongue demanded her response and she gave it, crushed beneath him until she was breathless. Only then did she let go, and the fear went away as he held her close, whispering in her ear. She inhaled his body heat, the aftershave, his breath on her face, felt the power of his long and vital limbs enclose her.

He was just as he always had been, a beautiful, sensual being, and nothing on earth or in heaven could change the way she felt about him. Her body longed to be satisfied. Her stomach cramped with need.

'Do you know what you're doing to me?' he demanded hoarsely.

She knew exactly, and wove her hands over his hips and thighs and the smooth, flat plane of his abdomen. Then trickled them down further until she found what she had been searching for.

'Oh, Alex…not yet.'

But it had to be. She was too eager, too desperate, too hungry. Need was erupting inside her and she couldn't hide it.

'Daniel…don't make me wait. Please.'

He gave a groan and closed his eyes. Their bodies were on fire and needed satisfaction. Then he flicked open his lids and she saw the raw hunger.

'Just a little longer…' he assured her, and exquisitely, wonderfully, he stroked and cajoled her, sending little convulsions of joy over her skin. His rhythm was perfect, his hands guiding her expertly. Her fingers tunnelled through his hair and over the sweat-beaded skin of his neck.

Sensual, wanton thoughts flashed in and out of her mind. His touch coaxed more and more from her. She melted and burned and throbbed, every part of her wanting him, waiting for the sensation of his fingers. His hips trapped her, and as he slid into her the thrust took her upwards and held her captive. He kept her there, recognising her need and denying it until at last she cried out again.

Then he took her suddenly. Her mind jettisoned and he came with her, suppressing the moan in his throat until he drove them both to the final peak. It lasted an eternity, yet seemed over too quickly, and he held her against him. She felt the fire warm them then, the aftermath soothe them, and he sank beside her, wrapping her in his arms.

She shuddered and pillowed her head on his shoulder. Tenderly he kissed her, her lips bruised and moist and utterly satisfied. Running his hands down, he lifted the sheet and dragged it over them, and they lay at perfect peace.

Later, he made love to her again. Voluptuously, sensually. He satisfied every need. This time she didn't plead for release. She waited, coaxing him as he had coaxed her. Instinctively, passionately, provocatively, she made love to him. And she knew that it would never be so fulfilling, so perfect—ever—with another human being.

When it was over they slept briefly, his arms locked round hers. She even managed to dream. Sleek, soft, warm dreams that were too erotic to acknowledge. She felt herself growing aroused in her sleep.

Then suddenly she woke; a noise was coming from somewhere in the house. 'It's my mother,' she whispered, and he started beside her.

'Oh, hell,' he muttered, holding her still. 'I didn't mean to fall asleep. What time is it?'

'Late, I expect. The movie must be over.'

'What do we do now?'

'Nothing.' A lazy smile tugged at her lips. 'Mum isn't likely to come in.'

'No, but I would give her the fright of her life if we met in the middle of the night on the way to the loo.'

She licked her lips, stretching under him like a lazy cat. 'Mum wouldn't mind. You know that.'

'No, but I do. For Helen and Cossie's sakes.'

She sighed softly, curling her legs over his and tracing her finger over his lips. The tiny scar was almost invisible now. It seemed light years since the fire, and that morning Peter had come in to say that Daniel was involved. She had known then how deeply she cared for him, but she'd tried to convince herself that she didn't. And now they were lovers.

Again.

'Alex, I have to go,' he told her softly, and she nodded miserably. His lovely dark hair was ruffled and she sank her face against it, inhaling his smell. It made her shudder, and he held tightly before easing her gently away. 'Is there some way I can leave without embarrassing Helen?'

'I suppose.' She nodded reluctantly. 'I'll go down. You can slip out of the front door.'

'Is the gate to the garden unlocked?'

'Why?'

'I came on foot, through the forest and the back garden.'

She folded her arms around him. 'Had you planned on seducing me?'

He rolled her on her back and kissed her slowly. 'Of course not.'

'I'm not sure that I believe you—'

'Stop it. Where are my clothes?'

She felt her heart contract a little, knew he was going. 'On the floor, where you left them.'

He threw back the sheets and swung his legs out of bed. She watched his long, lean body slip noiselessly across the room and into his clothes. Following him, she found her robe and wrapped it round her.

'Come here,' he told her, and pulled her into his arms. He smelt of lovemaking and the bittersweet tang of aftershave. She inhaled, closing her eyes, and clung to him. Something heavy and hurtful weighed inside her and she knew she was missing him already.

'I don't want tonight to be over. Don't go.'

'Alex, this is difficult enough.' He kissed the top of her head and held her away. 'I'm not made of cast-iron.'

She nodded, looking under her lids. 'See you tomorrow, then.'

'No—because I told Ollie I would still be away.'

She sighed and bit her lip. 'When?'

'Tuesday morning. I'm scheduled for a surgery and you have one too.' He held her face between his hands and smiled. 'Now, go do your stuff. I'm relying on you for cover. And make certain the front door's unlocked.'

'All right,' she murmured, and he kissed her one last time. Then she opened the door. 'Wait for my voice. I'll keep Mum in the kitchen.'

As she left he blew her a kiss. It was the last thing she saw and she would remember it for days. The gesture, the look in his eyes, the ache in her chest—and the longing she had to hide as she went downstairs to greet her mother.

CHAPTER ELEVEN

TERRY HALL'S house lay back from the road. When Alex drove past it she strained to see in. The drive was a riot of laurel and only the tip of the roof was visible. She was late, so she resisted the urge to stop, forcing her concentration back to the road.

She wished that she'd got up earlier. She'd slept so deeply. And this morning she hadn't wanted to get up. Daniel's aroma lingered on her pillow and in the sheets. So she'd hugged herself dreamily and thought about last night, ached to see him again.

Hold him…touch him.

She'd made herself late and showered in a hurry, grateful Ollie was taking Cossie to school. Helen had slept late too, and hadn't come down for breakfast, and Alex's hand had hovered on the telephone in the kitchen.

She'd wanted to hear his voice—just once. Just to make certain she hadn't dreamt it all. But the feeling inside her was proof enough. Her body felt glowing. Her thoughts ranged from euphoric to dismayed, but she didn't want to analyse anything this morning. She felt gloriously content and the little voice of warning was conveniently silent.

She hadn't phoned in the end, just promised herself she would later.

The morning was sunny and bright—a Christmas morning. The girls hadn't put up the tree in the surgery, but cards were flowing in. They lined the shelves and walls, and someone had strung tinsel and a few holly leaves.

'The children were fine,' Ollie told her hurriedly in the office. 'Thanks for letting me borrow Cossie. Emma seemed so much better.'

144

'Did you manage to talk to her about Grant?' Alex asked as she collected her mail from the desk.

'No. But I will tonight, when we're on our own.'

'Okay. Well, I'd better get started. Who's first in?'

'Julie Dingle—followed by a tragically long list, I'm afraid. Without Dr Hayward we're a bit swamped. Still, he said he'll be back tomorrow—or even tonight.'

Alex hoped Ollie didn't notice her blush and hurried to her room. It was hopeless trying to concentrate on the mail. Daniel intruded into her thoughts—the way he'd held her and touched her last night. She hadn't even asked him about his trip to London. She supposed that deep in her heart she didn't really want to know. It was as though she'd fallen back into an old trap.

'I didn't think I'd feel like Christmas at all,' her first patient, Julie Dingle, commented. 'But I do.'

'You've changed your job?' Alex guessed.

'No, but Sue, your nurse, gave me those counselling videos. I've read some books too—and, well...I've learnt a lot.' Julie's cheeks went red and Alex wondered what her fiancé's response had been. After a pause, Julie added hesitantly, 'I think I was just using my migraines as an excuse not to have sex.'

'Have you spoken to Tim about it?'

She nodded. 'We've discussed it, rather than fought over it. I told him I wanted to get our problems sorted out or not get married at all. He watched the videos with me. One of the things they explain is that women want romance and not just sex. Tim got quite a shock. He didn't realise how much I still needed that, even though we've been living together for five years.'

'Has that made a difference to your relationship?'

Julie paused. 'I think so. We're both trying harder. What I'd like to do now is stop taking the Pill. I've been on it for six years and I think that's one of the things I worry about.'

By the time Julie left Alex had discussed the alternatives

and suggested that Tim be involved in her decision too. Alex hoped they'd make it. They were trying hard enough, and Julie had focused on issues that couples often failed to discuss before marriage. Five years was a long-term relationship. But marriage was longer.

A thought that appeared to have occurred to Jane Glynn when she walked into her surgery with her husband Martin.

'I want the biopsy,' she told Alex quietly. 'I just hope it's not too late.'

'What changed your mind?' Alex asked.

'Something Dr Hayward said to Martin. He was referring to his shingles. He said the nervous system takes a body blow but so does the ego—because shingles is so often associated with ageing.'

Alex nodded slowly. 'And you related to that?'

Jane nodded. 'If I had to have a breast removed—perhaps both—what would be left? I have no womb and no ovaries— what's the point of being a woman?' She looked up at her husband. 'And yet suddenly there was every reason. I want to live—very much.'

'How soon could Jane go in?' Martin asked Alex.

'Is the lump any larger?'

'I don't think so...' Jane hesitated.

Alex stood up. 'Let's check you, then, and we'll take it from there.' Alex examined her and the lump was still there, lurking under her right breast on the bra line.

'I'll ring Mr Brace,' Alex told her. 'They'll either write to you or, if you've a contact number, I'll ask them to ring.'

'I'm sorry,' Jane apologised as she slipped on her coat. 'I should never have hesitated.'

'I'll tell Mr Brace what you told me,' Alex replied, and looked at Jane's husband. 'How are you feeling now?'

'Better now that Jane's changed her mind.' He smiled. 'Thanks, Dr Trent.'

The couple went off hand in hand and Alex sat for a while thinking about them. Jane had told her as she'd been examined that she felt less of a woman. Fear of loss of femininity was an issue that women rarely addressed directly.

It had taken Jane some time to put it together. But she'd seen the connection between her husband's stress-related problems and his shingles. Because she cared for him she had been able to put his welfare before hers. An irony, since it had brought her back to square one and the importance of her own health issues.

It was something that Alex had noticed over the years. Concern for a loved one's health was often greater than personal worry. Daniel had been concerned for his parents all those years ago. He'd made exhausting trips back home to see his ailing father and their own relationship had suffered because of it.

Had she been more mature, would she have understood Daniel's actions? Maybe. But she'd been so hungry for him that she'd seen it as rejection, thought their relationship hadn't been important to him. They'd wanted their medical careers so badly. Perhaps they'd wanted it all—too much, too quickly. Daniel had been just off his Finals and she a mere second-year student.

Alex closed her eyes and pushed her hands over her face. The memories were all too clear. Love hadn't conquered all. She'd been resentful and demanding. And had eventually offered an ultimatum. Could she blame Daniel for leaving her? For choosing not to make the choice between her and his parents? Would she do that now? If they could go back nine years, would she still give Daniel that same ultimatum?

Alex shook her head, as if to clear the thoughts, then turned to the phone and lifted it. 'Pauline, who's next?' she asked quickly.

'Dr Trent—I was just going to buzz you,' the receptionist said hesitantly. 'Can you pop out for a moment?'

'Is there a problem?'

'Well, you've a visitor—and as you're in the middle of surgery—'

'Okay. I'll come right away.'

Alex went to the office and found Pauline behind the reception desk. When she saw Alex her eyes slewed to the waiting room. Alex followed her gaze to the slight, boyish figure dressed entirely in black leather. Pacing energetically up and down, speaking on a mobile phone, Zak had taken the waiting room by storm.

'Sorry to interrupt you,' Pauline said, and lifted her shoulders.

Alex felt her heart bounce, then drop like a lead weight as Zak turned and spotted her, raising his hand—and the mobile—in dramatic salute.

In the spilt second it took her to respond, she realised she had two options. And she had to make her decision before Zak took over the whole building.

The first was to shepherd him into the office. The second, into her room. If they used the office the waiting patients and staff would be able to see and hear everything. Yet if she took him into her room she'd be trapped.

But then the figure hurdled across the line of outstretched legs and disappeared. 'Thanks, Pauline,' Alex said hurriedly over her shoulder as she grappled for the door-handle. 'Tell my next patient I'll be a few minutes.'

As she opened the door Zak was standing there. 'Allie—honey!'

'Hi,' she managed. 'This is a surprise. I thought you were going to phone.'

'Yeah—I should've. Hey, you look great.' She closed the door quickly, but as she turned back he pulled her into his arms. 'Happy Christmas,' he whispered, and almost twirled her off her feet.

Her heart sank as she realised he was going to throw their lives upside-down! 'Thought I'd give you a surprise. Allie, you look fantastic.' He planted a kiss on her mouth, and she was in the process of regaining her balance when she saw the figure at the end of the hall.

Daniel stood watching them, though how long he had been there she didn't know. Then Zak caught her arms again and gave her a little shake, recapturing her attention.

'Can you get away, honey?'

'Zak, I'm in the middle of surgery!'

'So it's a no?'

'Of course it is.' She smoothed down her ruffled clothing and looked back along the hall. The tall figure had gone. Alex closed her eyes and gulped a breath, then she looked back at Zak.

A mischievous grin spread from ear to ear and dark eyes twinkled under the mop of untidy hair. When Zak looked at her like that he was so much like Cossie she couldn't be cross with him for long.

'Have you hired a car?' she asked needlessly.

'Sure. It's outside.'

'Cossie's still at school. It would be nice if you could collect him. I'll phone school and let them know.'

'Okay.' Zak shrugged easily. 'Then we'll come here, right?'

'Wrong,' she told him patiently. 'Go home with Cossie, spend some time with him. He misses you, you know.'

'I know, doll, but I'll make it up to him,' Zak promised her, looking like a chastened bloodhound.

'I'll join you as soon as I can.'

Zak nodded and mimicked a salute. Then before she could move he was hugging her again, and Alex finally succumbed. Zak hadn't grown up yet. He probably never would.

All she had to do now was explain that to Daniel.

Which wasn't as easy as it sounded.

Anyone who knew Zak, and the crazy world he lived in, might understand. But for the normal person Zak was an enigma.

All you've got to do, she told herself throughout the afternoon, is explain that he's totally irrepressible. Kissing her meant nothing. She could have been one of the patients.

And it was Christmas—almost. Partying ran in Zak's blood. He'd be uncontainable for the next few weeks. Which was great, because his mood would stretch into the New Year, and then he'd be off into some other part of the universe. There'd be no downside.

Lord knew where he'd go! But a card would plop through the letterbox or the phone would ring in the middle of the night. After an indecipherable few words he'd ring off and then she'd have to try to get back to sleep.

Yes, easy enough to explain. That little display in the hall had meant nothing. Why, oh, why had Daniel had to appear at that moment? He was supposed to be away.

Before she left, she spoke to Pauline.

'Um, where's Dr Hayward?' she said tentatively as she dragged on her coat.

'He popped by, but didn't stay.'

'I thought I saw him in the hall.'

Pauline frowned as she turned from the desk. 'Yes, he was coming to see you, he said. Then he shot out again. He must have forgotten something.'

'Yes, probably,' Alex mumbled. 'Anyway, I'll catch up with him tomorrow. I'm off now, Pauline.'

But before she could leave the phone rang in the office and Pauline answered it. 'Dr Trent—it's for you.'

The voice on the other end was Gail's. 'Stephen's being discharged tomorrow,' she told Alex excitedly. 'They want to keep an eye on him, so he's got an outpatients appointment next week. But we can handle that.'

'That's wonderful news, Gail. Let me know how things go, will you?'

'Oh, yes, don't worry. Stephen's had a lot of thinking time. Me too. I'll keep you posted.'

Alex drove home past their cottage and felt happy for the

couple. They deserved a little luck. Their way of life wasn't easy or glamorous, but they'd stuck to it and to each other.

She soon forgot about Gail and Stephen as she opened the front door. A wild guitar was playing upstairs, the hall was a mess and it was clear Zak was in full swing. She promised herself that as soon as she could she'd ring Daniel. Explaining over the phone would be tough. Still, she'd never get to see him tonight.

Alex trod over the mountain of luggage and bags and found Helen in the kitchen, juggling supper. 'Sorry,' she sighed, and kissed her mother's cheek. 'Zak just turned up, as usual, with not so much as a phone call, so I couldn't let you know.'

'Don't worry, darling. At least I had his room ready.'

'Yes, but he should have phoned.'

'That's Zak,' Helen said bravely. 'I've prepared salad, cold meat and hot bread. What about pudding?'

'Anything.' Alex shrugged as Zak's laughter echoed. 'What can I do to help?'

Helen gave her napkins and cutlery. 'Set the table—then we'll eat. And before I forget—' A sudden blast from the stereo system shook the house and Helen paused. 'Daniel phoned earlier today. He said he'd call round this evening. But then he rang again and said he'd leave it.'

'What time was that?'

'About four, I think.'

Just after he'd seen her with Zak. Alex felt her heart drop to her boots. But her mother was staring at her and she gave a little shrug. 'It's probably better he decided not to come,' she managed.

'Yes, but—' Helen began, only to be drowned out again.

'I'll turn it down,' Alex shouted. When she arrived in the big front room Zak was sprawled against the sofa, talking to—no, Alex corrected herself, talking *at* Cossie.

Even Cossie looked mindblown as he curled on the sofa.

Zak was handing him photos and Cossie's little face was puckered in a frown.

The television was on, but the sound was turned down. Music from the stereo thudded through the walls and Cossie's favourite programme was ending.

Alex turned down the stereo and flipped off the TV. She tried to swallow her irritation; Cossie saw Zak so rarely she ought to be able to cope. But this time it was harder to deal with.

Zak had intruded on her private life. A life she obviously wasn't supposed to have. A life that didn't matter, that held as little interest for Zak as the weather forecast.

Daniel, she thought longingly, where are you? You should be here. With us. You should be here, sitting with Cossie, as you used to. Laughing and joking about something in Cossie's small but important life.

Was it only last night they'd made love? The memory of him was still fresh in her mind. The smell of his delicious body, the sound of his voice, the feel of his hair-roughened skin. They'd made no promises, said nothing about today, but she needed to have his arms around her. To be reassured last night hadn't been a dream.

But he's leaving, the little voice argued inside her. He's going away. And it's useless to think he's not. Maybe they'd never see each other again...

There had been a spark of hope last night. A senseless but delicious, promising spark. Enough to get her through today, until she saw him again.

Now she wouldn't.

Zak's arrival had condemned them to be apart. She looked at Zak and for the first time realised how selfish and thoughtless he was, with as little regard for her and his son as he had for other people's lives. He was oblivious to Cossie's pale and silent little form as he leaned against the sofa and rattled off his adventures.

Poor Cossie!

How must he feel, looking at those photographs? It was another world and he wasn't part of it. Zak only ever took him to London, and then he abandoned the child—disappearing for days on end whilst Cossie was entertained by his grandparents.

Zak was telling him about the people he'd met, the places he's stayed and Cossie was his audience. That was all. An audience. Something to be worshipped by.

'Supper's almost ready,' Alex said with sudden passion. 'Zak, perhaps you'd like to lay the table?'

The father of her child stopped midstream. He stared up at her. She'd never asked him that kind of question before and she almost laughed. Not at herself, for asking it. But at Zak's expression. His jaw had dropped.

'You know where the dining room is?'

Cossie wriggled in his seat and looked up at her. 'Can I help, Mum?'

'You bet. Run and ask Grandma.'

Cossie leapt off the sofa and disappeared. The photos slid off the cushions and onto the floor and Alex dropped the napkins beside them.

Then walked out.

It was late in the evening before Alex managed to phone Daniel. Cossie was in bed asleep, and Zak and Helen had taken Suzie for a walk. She settled herself in the study and dialed Terry Hall's number.

Her heart was beating a tattoo in her chest, and when he didn't pick up she felt desolate.

Ten o'clock. It wasn't too late. Where was he? By the time Zak and Helen returned she'd tried three times. Could she justify another call from her room?

But if Daniel had wanted to speak to her he would have been there. She showered and struggled to decide, and finally went to bed at midnight. She still had an impossible hope that he'd phone, even at that late hour.

But he didn't. And she eventually fell asleep in the small hours. Her dreams were filled with anxiety, and when she woke she remembered Zak was in the house. And that she hadn't spoken to Daniel. Hadn't been able to explain, or touch, or kiss...

She left after breakfast, and Zak took Cossie to school. There were promises that he'd collect him too, but Alex wasn't certain.

'You might get caught up,' she'd reminded him before she left. 'It's happened before.'

'No worries, honey. Promise.'

She'd left it at that, but she was anxious all day. A day in which the briefest glimpse of Daniel made her heart leap. But it was nightmarishly busy. Another flu bug was winging its way through the town. Pre-Christmas, everyone panicked.

'Dr Hayward's on call,' Ollie told her as she looked in the office. 'Dr Barlow and Dr Ashley are taking surgeries till one. We've an emergency list as long as your arm. Can I pop one or two in with you?'

Alex nodded. 'Has Dr Hayward left any messages?'

Ollie shook her head. 'Oh, Dr Trent, I spoke to Emma last night. I told her about Grant moving, and his new house with more rooms. I explained she would be as much a part of his life as she always has been.' Ollie smiled. 'We both shed a few tears. But this morning she seemed a lot happier.'

'I'm glad, Ollie.'

'Do you want me to send your first one in?'

'Yes, and a coffee afterwards would be really welcome.'

'Oh, look—Dr Hayward's just coming back...'

Alex turned and came face to face with Daniel as he walked in the office. Her heart gave a rickety little row of beats, then seemed suspended in mid-air as he met her gaze. His grey eyes were darker than she had ever seen them and shadows hollowed the spaces underneath. He looked tired, and yet so stunningly handsome that all she wanted to do was throw her arms around him.

'Hi, Alex.'

'Daniel…I thought I'd missed you.'

'I left—but got halfway there and realised I didn't have Mrs Jeeves's notes.'

'Oh, didn't I give them to you, Dr Hayward?' Ollie turned the carousel and slipped them out. 'Sorry. It was the last call and we've been crazy here.'

'That's okay, Ollie.' He grabbed them and slipped them into his overcoat pocket. Then he looked at Alex and shrugged lightly. 'Sorry, I have to rush.'

'Okay—will I see you when you get back?' Alex faltered, taking a chance that Ollie wouldn't hear as she dealt with patients at the desk. 'I need to speak to you.'

He gave her a glance that was impossible to understand. Not unless she wanted to look on the black side. And she didn't. She wanted things the way they'd been on Sunday. She wanted him in her arms and kissing her, even if it was temporary, and she wanted the rest of the world to go away.

'I'll try to look in when I get back,' he told her, then tacked a smile on his lips. 'See you.'

It was nothing—just a hint of smile—but she clung to the hope of it all morning. Despite a call from Zak and the impatience of her patients, who wanted to be well for Christmas, Alex survived the day.

At the end of it she still hadn't seen Daniel. Then, just as she finished, Ollie rang through on the internal phone.

'Dr Trent, Mrs Jeeves has just rung. She's not feeling very well.'

'Didn't Dr Hayward see her today?'

'Yes, this morning. She's got flu and he was going back this evening to check on her. I don't know whether to ring Dr Hayward because ten minutes ago he was helping with a road traffic accident on the outskirts of town.'

'Don't bother him, Ollie. I'll go. I'm all finished here.'

'Oh, thanks, Dr Trent. I'll ring her back.'

Alex pulled on her coat and grabbed her bag. In less than

ten minutes she had turned the corner to Mrs Jeeves's road. They were all old Victorian houses and Alex knew from previous visits that the one she wanted was in a middle terraced row.

The light wasn't on in the window and the lace curtains hung bleakly in the winter darkness. Alex tapped on the door but drew no response. There was an alley at the side of the next house. She followed it and found the back gardens. Turning right at the end, she saw a little row of gates lined the lane. Mrs Jeeves's gate swung open with a creak and Alex hurried up the darkened path to the back door.

It was open. The house was in darkness, so she flicked on the lights as she went through. She remembered Mrs Jeeves's sitting room and it was there she checked first. It was a sad little sight: a few Christmas cards dotted on shelves, old-fashioned furniture and a faded picture gallery over the fireplace.

'Mrs Jeeves?' Alex called, and searched the rest of downstairs. Then, just as she was going up, someone knocked on the front door.

It was Daniel. 'Alex, I saw your car. What are you doing here?'

She explained, but he looked puzzled. 'I don't understand.' He frowned. 'She has flu symptoms and a chest infection but nothing too serious. She was sitting down here when I left—' He stopped and they looked at each other.

Together they hurdled the stairs; Daniel searched the front, Alex the back. 'Here!' Daniel called, and Alex felt her heart pound. She ran to the front bedroom and found Daniel standing by the big double bed. Mrs Jeeves lay there, unmoving.

'Oh, no,' Alex whispered, and came to stand beside him.

'No pulse, but she's warm.'

'I drove straight here,' Alex protested. 'I couldn't have been ten minutes. Ollie phoned her to say I was coming.'

'The bed's too spongy for CPR,' Daniel said hurriedly,

stripping off his coat and opening his case. 'Let's have her down on the floor.'

Alex threw off her coat and they lifted the tiny little form to the floor. Daniel administered adrenaline and they worked together with chest compressions.

'And again,' Daniel said urgently, and they tried until Alex felt the sweat bead her spine.

'It's useless, I'm afraid,' Daniel said eventually. 'We're too late.'

For a moment Alex held her breath and waited, as if expecting a miracle. But then Daniel got up slowly and came to stand behind her. She felt his hands on her shoulders, tugging her up. 'Come on, we've done everything we can.'

'But it's Christmas,' Alex whispered hoarsely. 'It doesn't seem fair.'

'Has she any family?'

'A son, I think. In Tyllington. We've got a contact number.' Alex bit her lip. 'When I saw her last, she said—' She stopped then. She couldn't tell Daniel what Mrs Jeeves had said. *'I may be old, and a little deaf, but I can still recognise an adoring male when I see one.'*

'Said what, Alex?'

'Just how busy our practice seemed. Like her father's.'

'He was a GP?'

'No, a vet. From the Midlands, I think.'

They stood in silence for a few moments, then Daniel hunkered down. 'We'll restore her to bed, then make some calls.'

Finally Alex went downstairs. She found the phone on a little table by the hearth, together with a bundle of knitting. Beside it was a photo of a young bride and groom, old and well-thumbed and detached from its frame. Had Mrs Jeeves been looking at it before going upstairs? They'd never know.

Alex said a swift little prayer, stabbed the numbers and cleared her throat before speaking.

Gareth Jeeves arrived later, a stout, middle-aged man with alarmed blue eyes. They explained how they'd tried CPR and hadn't been able to revive her. He nodded in a daze and went upstairs, and then Daniel's mobile rang.

'A new mum with flu,' he told her as he flipped it off. 'The baby's not too bright either. I'll have to go.'

Alex hesitated. She had to say something before he went. 'Daniel…this isn't the right time, I know, but—Zak's home.'

His face was unreadable. 'I gathered as much.'

'I tried to ring you last night. I wanted to explain about yesterday, in the hall—'

'Alex, it's okay,' he interrupted her. 'I've no intention of making things awkward for you, if that's what you're worried about.'

Alex stared at him in astonishment. 'That's not what I meant—'

'*Alex.*' He stopped her, opening the front door. 'I really do have to go.'

'But when I can see you?' she tried again. 'Maybe later?'

He looked at her, his face slightly twisted, and then a creak on the stairs made her spin round.

'Can you tell me what happened?' Gareth Jeeves asked, looking bewildered.

'Dr Trent will tell you as much as we know,' Daniel said quickly. 'I'm afraid I'm on call and have a patient to see. Again, my condolences, Mr Jeeves.' And with shoulders hunched he turned away. Alex stood watching him, wondering if she'd imagined what he'd said.

'Dr Trent?' Gareth Jeeves was staring at her. 'Was it a heart attack?'

She swallowed and nodded. 'Probably—though we won't know for certain just yet.'

'Was it quick, do you think?'

The sound of an engine broke the silence outside. She closed the door and leaned against it. 'Yes, I believe so.'

'I…I just never thought about this happening. She was

always so independent. She was always—well, *here*.' A little hitch caught in his throat.

'Let's have some tea,' she murmured, and led the way to the kitchen. When she'd made tea they sat at the table and she tried to concentrate on listening to Mrs Jeeves's dismayed son. It wasn't easy. Daniel's cold indifference made her shudder; he'd clearly not wanted an explanation.

'You're her only son?' she asked distractedly.

'The only child, yes. I should have done more, I suppose. I only live a few streets away. I feel—well, I don't know how I feel. Except that I know it's too late to change things.'

'Did you want to?' Alex asked curiously.

'Yes. I just never got round to it. I'd call at Christmas, and her birthday, do a bit of shopping occasionally. My wife called in sometimes. I told myself it was enough. With a family and a demanding job it's difficult.'

'I'm sure she understood.'

Gareth Jeeves heaved a sigh. 'I'd better get cracking. Arrangements to make and so forth.' He stood up, took his mug to the sink, washed it and looked out of the window. Suddenly his head dropped and his shoulders shook and Alex quietly left him to grieve.

She barely spoke to Daniel the rest of the week. Not because she didn't want to—she ached to. When she saw him, he was polite, but said no more than he had to. So she struggled through and hoped for an opportunity.

But one never came, and by the end of the week she'd given up. The flu continued, despite the vaccination programme, and surgeries were endless.

On Friday she had a surprise when she arrived early at the surgery. Gail and Stephen Hurd were sitting in the waiting room. Stephen looked pale and thinner, but he was smiling. 'We came to say thank you,' he told her, stretching out his hand, and Alex grasped it and felt the strength in his fingers.

'You're okay?' she asked delightedly.

'Thanks to you and Dr Hayward. Is he around?'

Alex shook her head. 'Not yet. It's a little early.'

'Well, then—' he chuckled '—just tell him there's no way I'll be scything fern again. It was that stuff that caused the allergic reaction, just as he said.'

Alex smiled. 'It was a mystery at first, but I'm glad it's solved.'

'And there's this,' Gail said quietly, glancing down at the glistening ring on her finger. 'We're engaged.' She met Alex's eyes and there was a message there that Alex understood.

'Wonderful news.' Alex smiled. 'When are you getting married?'

'Next year,' Gail murmured, glancing at the man beside her. 'And we're planning a honeymoon abroad.' She turned to Alex and grinned. 'So if you want to stay in a Commoner's cottage for two weeks and really get back to nature, you're welcome.'

Alex feigned shock and pulled a face. 'Thanks for the offer, but I know just how hard getting back to nature must be. It's not quite as easy as it looks on the TV, is it?'

They all laughed, and spoke a few moments longer before Alex's patients began to arrive. After the couple had gone she thought about how Stephen and Gail had finally made it. Gail's eyes had been filled with true happiness and she deserved it. It was through her determination that the relationship had survived.

Alex reflected again on what had happened between her and Daniel almost a decade ago. She'd loved him to distraction. But she'd been too young to be able to compromise and had offered him that fateful ultimatum.

It was almost too painful to think about, and she began surgery, grateful for the problems of her patients, which inevitably put life into perspective.

That evening, before she left, Peter joined her in the office.

'The call register's not up yet.' He frowned as he glanced at the noticeboard. 'Who's on this weekend?'

'I am,' Alex replied—and thank God, she thought. Zak was a dear, but he'd never lost the need to be occupied.

'But haven't you got company?' Peter protested. 'I'll take it, if you like. You look tired, Alex.'

'I'm okay.' She smiled. 'But thanks.'

'How long is Zak staying?' he asked curiously.

'I'm not sure,' she admitted. 'Christmas-ish, I think.' Alex arched an eyebrow. 'He's waiting for news from an agency in London. Some kind of band promo deal.' She paused and grinned. 'You know Zak.'

'I do indeed,' Peter said wryly. 'But you're on duty over Christmas. Are you sure can handle it?'

'Standing on my head,' she told him lightly. 'It'll be great for Cossie if Zak's here. Anyway, I volunteered for Christmas, remember?'

'Crazy lady.' Peter chuckled and held open the door. 'If you change your mind, Daniel's offered to take it.'

Alex paused, her brow tightening in a frown. 'Has he? Any reason?'

Peter grimaced as they walked out into the night. 'Well, yes. Don't you know?'

Alex folded her bag over her arm and realised her hands weren't steady. Her legs had the weird sort of jelly feeling that accompanied shock. Not that she'd had one yet, but she could feel one about to come.

And it did.

Peter licked his top lip anxiously. 'Alex, he's leaving.'

She shook her head slowly. 'Leaving?'

'At the end of January. The job offer from London? The African project? He's accepted.' Peter's face crumpled. 'Oh, Alex. I'm sorry. You really didn't know, did you?'

'No,' she whispered. 'I didn't.' They stood still for a few seconds until Peter took her arm and urged her forward.

'Come on. I'll walk with you to your car.'

Alex nodded, walking in a trance. She felt the icy wind whip her face and trickle down inside her collar. Her muscles tensed. Her bones felt frozen.

But it was nothing to the coldness that gripped her heart.

CHAPTER TWELVE

THE weekend provided distraction enough. A premature baby girl was born in the early hours of Saturday. The father was away and the woman had rung Alex in a panic. The birth was quick and Alex saw mother and child into hospital.

Luckily, mother and baby were soon blooming, and Alex arrived home in the wee small hours. She wondered if she dared grab sleep and she did. Five hours. Then she was out again, throwing on trousers and a warm sweater and driving to a farm on the outskirts of Tyllington.

A thirteen-year-old had been vomiting and kept his ragged parents up all night. Alex eliminated appendicitis and meningitis. Then trusted her nose. A hangover.

The worried mother swore her son had never drunk alcohol. But when she left the room Alex asked him if he had. At first it was a no, then he nodded, feeling too ill to pretend.

He said it was the first time and Alex believed him. He vowed he'd never do it again and pleaded with her not to tell his mother.

She struck a deal, saying she wouldn't—this time. He was an intelligent boy, so she pointed out the dangers and drew a smile, then left him with plenty to think about. The mother seemed satisfied with a tummy upset, and was reassured when Alex said he'd be better by the evening.

When she got home Helen was loading the washing machine. 'Zak's phone call came through,' she paused to tell her. 'He's leaving on Monday and wants to take Cossie.'

'To his parents?' Alex asked needlessly.

'So I gather.'

'I'll have to ring school. It's the last week of term.'

'I'm sure they won't mind.' Helen shrugged. 'And Zak's

promised to have him back for Christmas.' Helen raised her eyes. 'He's upstairs making calls. He told me to tell you that he's booking a table and taking us out to celebrate tomorrow night. A thank-you meal, he said. For being so patient. Though I expect going out will be the last thing you'll fancy. I know you'll be shattered.'

'Oh, never mind,' Alex sighed. 'At least we know where we stand now.' She looked around, realising the house was quiet. 'Where's Cossie?'

'Marcus's mother called. She had a hack organised for Marcus and there was a place spare. Cossie said he'd like to go, so she came and collected him. I didn't think you'd mind.'

'Of course not. But I'm surprised,' Alex admitted as they went back into the kitchen. 'I thought he'd want to be with Zak.'

Helen gave a little chuckle. 'I think a hack had considerably more allure,' she whispered. 'Now, let me make us some coffee.'

Alex sat down at the table with a sigh and blinked her eyes.

'Busy night?' Helen asked as she started the percolator.

'A premature baby and an adolescent with a hangover.'

Helen raised her eyebrows. 'Do hangovers warrant visits these days?'

'Only if you're thirteen, experimenting, and terrified of what your parents will say.' She smiled softly. 'He said it was his first time. I gave him the benefit of the doubt.'

'Lucky lad.'

'He was a nice little chap. I think he's learnt a valuable lesson. He talked to me—that was something. If he'd shut up like a clam and glowered I might have had second thoughts.'

'Oh, that reminds me,' Helen said quickly as she shuffled the mugs, 'Daniel rang. He asked if you'd phone him. He's at home—or should be.'

For a moment Alex stared at her mother, then grew wings on her feet. Suddenly the world seemed to have righted itself. It wasn't the dark, cold place that had enveloped her as she trudged through the gloom this morning. It was bright and beautiful again, and Daniel wanted to speak to her.

She grabbed the phone, heard Zak on the line and replaced it. Two minutes later she tried again.

'Daniel,' she gulped breathlessly. 'It's Alex.'

'Hi,' he said coolly, and her heart tipped. 'I know you're busy. But I wondered if you're free tomorrow evening.'

Her heart did a complete somersault. 'Yes,' she said, without thinking, then clapped a hand to her mouth. 'Oh, goodness. I would be, but Zak's arranged a meal…he's taking Cossie to London, you see—'

He stopped her. 'No problem. I wanted to tell you that I'm leaving. I thought we might have spent an hour together. But it doesn't matter.' His voice faded whilst a terrified little voice of her own, deep inside her head, screamed *no*. 'Anyway, I've told you now, so that's okay,' he said with finality.

'Daniel, I'd like to see you,' she flustered miserably. Her head was spinning. 'One evening after work?'

The long silence told her he was thinking. 'Maybe,' he settled for, and she felt sick. 'Look, I have to go. Terry's here. I'm helping him crate up his photographs for an exhibition.' He paused. 'Enjoy yourself tomorrow.'

She stood with the phone in her hand and the little click of finality made her shattered nerves jump. He'd seemed so cold, so distant, and tears pricked her eyes.

'Allie, honey?'

She looked up and saw Zak on the stairs. 'How long have you been there?' she croaked.

He didn't reply, but padded down the stairs in jeans and bare feet. She held her breath, trying not to blub.

'I'm sorry, babe,' he murmured, and patted her shoulder. 'Is this the Daniel you knew before us?'

'Mmm,' she managed, afraid to speak lest she make a fool of herself.

Zak grinned boyishly. 'Cossie says he's cool.'

'Does he? What did he say?'

'He likes animals and stuff. And Cossie's into that,' Zak said with hopeless simplicity.

She wondered if he secretly resented Daniel's presence in their son's life, but she didn't think so. Zak wasn't the type to get hung up on relationships. The one he had with himself was priority, and always would be. She found herself smiling. Zak's blind optimism was incredible.

'Want to talk?' Zak asked her, and she smiled.

'No. Tell me about Monday.'

She didn't need to ask twice. Zak wheeled her from the hall, clearly relieved he'd not encountered an emotional minefield. She would never have expected him to understand but she was grateful for his sympathy.

They went into the kitchen and found Helen making coffee. It wasn't long before Zak was in full flow and they listened, though Alex barely heard a word.

She missed Daniel so much. The old Daniel—her Daniel— the one who had made love to her and made her feel so complete, as though she had been waiting for him all these years without knowing it. He was leaving her again—she'd tried to prepare herself for this moment, but she'd failed.

She sipped her coffee, grateful for its warmth, and reminded herself how lucky she was. Her relationship with Cossie's father had endured. As for her lover? Where was their relationship leading?

She had the sinking feeling it was going nowhere.

All Daniel really intended was to say goodbye.

They dined out lavishly at the little Italian on Sunday night. Zak entertained the whole restaurant as usual, and Alex tried not to resent not being with Daniel. On Monday she phoned the school, and at lunchtime came home to say goodbye. Zak was piling luggage into the boot of his hired car and Helen was making a flask.

'Miss you lots,' she told Cossie as she zipped up his jacket.

'Me too.'

'Have fun with Nanna and Pops.'

'Will I be home for Christmas?'

'Of course you will.'

Cossie grinned and hugged her, and she tucked an envelope in his pocket. 'Give this to Nanna for me. I'll ring this evening.'

She'd written a letter of thanks to Zak's parents. They adored Cossie and would give him a wonderful holiday, with or without their son's presence.

'See you soon, hon,' Zak promised her, and settled Cossie in the car.

'Drive carefully,' she told him, and he winked.

'Snail's pace.' He grinned. Then he started the car and they disappeared quickly into the lane.

Back in the house the phone was ringing and Alex rushed to answer it. 'Dr Trent—we've a crisis,' Ollie told her. 'Everyone's out and we've an overspill.'

'I'll be there,' Alex promised, and when she got there she realised Ollie hadn't exaggerated. The waiting room was buzzing.

'''Coughs and sneezes spread diseases'',' Pauline teased as she took Alex in a cup of tea and the records. 'And we've plenty to choose from this afternoon. Who do you want? We've slotted four in and three are hopeful waiters.'

Alex smiled ruefully. 'Surprise me.'

'Oh, I think we can manage that.' The receptionist crooked an eyebrow and left.

Alex began surgery, not stopping again until five. Pauline had been right; a mixture of coughs, colds and chest infections was the order of the day, and at the end of it there was a cluster of prescriptions to sign.

Finally she finished the paperwork and sat back and rested

her head against the top of her chair. She wondered if Daniel was in surgery still and the thought revived her. Perhaps she'd find the courage to mention their last conversation.

But when she went out his door was closed. So she lingered in the office and examined the Christmas cards until Peter came in and heaved a sigh of relief that the day was over. At last Daniel joined them, and Alex, experiencing a surge of relief, tried to make eye contact.

She felt a ripple go through her when he brushed her arm with his sleeve. And a bubble rose in her chest as he laughed, flicking his liquid grey gaze briefly her way. Her heart tilted and she had to stop herself from hoping too much, from reading all the wrong things into a glance.

But then he said he had to go and she panicked. She couldn't ask him when they might meet in front of Peter and Ollie, who was still at the desk. So she had to watch helplessly as he turned and lifted his case.

Don't go, she pleaded silently, don't go. There's so much to say and so little time to say it in.

But he smiled and said goodnight, avoiding her questioning gaze. When he'd gone it felt as though the bottom had dropped out of her world. Had he forgotten they were going to meet? He'd showed no hesitation in leaving and hadn't tried to talk to her privately. Was he avoiding her?

That evening Helen went out with Jean, and Alex rang Cossie in London. Even speaking to Cossie and his grandparents didn't help. Afterwards she curled on the bottom stair in the golden glow of the Christmas tree and waited for Daniel to ring.

He didn't.

And somehow she hadn't thought he would.

It was the bleakest of weeks. While everyone was preparing for Christmas and the streets of Tyllington were full of shoppers Alex had to summon up enthusiasm. Cossie was away and she needed to shop. He'd spotted a bike in a shop window on the night they'd dined out. Alex found it was still there and bought it, trying to imagine Cossie's face on Christmas morning.

'The garage?' Helen suggested for a hiding place. And they covered it in tinsel and a tied a huge red bow to the handlebars.

On Friday evening the girls organised a small party. Peter and Sean joined them in the staffroom and it looked festive and seasonal with all the decorations.

'Home for Christmas?' Sean asked her as they ate mince pies and drank Norfolk punch and the party got into gear.

'Yes,' Alex acknowledged, wondering if Daniel, who was on call, would return before the party ended. 'Cossie's been away, but he'll home by then.'

'I hear you're on duty,' Sean murmured, loudly crunching on nuts. 'What folly made you volunteer for Christmas?'

Alex smiled, her lovely blue eyes glued to the door. If she visualised hard enough, Daniel might come through it. 'I can't remember.' She shrugged. 'Maybe I thought it would get me the job.'

'Lord, girl, there would be no contest. Peter's wanted you from the word go. His biggest job was convincing you. And, besides, he wasn't sure about your back.'

'Whether I was ready to work?' Alex mused, tilting a pale eyebrow.

'Absolutely. That was a nasty tumble you took.'

'It seems so long ago now I can hardly remember,' Alex admitted as she sipped her drink. The punch was non-alcoholic, but it was zippy. She grimaced. 'Yeuch!'

Peter laughed. 'They should get a licence for this stuff.' He gulped it and smacked his lips. 'Hey, Daniel's back.'

Alex watched breathily as Sean leapt up to the worktop. He poured a glass of punch and handed it to Daniel. She couldn't take her eyes away. Daniel looked tall and gorgeous, his broad shoulders swinging out from under his coat as he tossed it over a chair. His dark hair had grown and curled over his collar, a beautiful contrast against the stark white of his shirt.

She took another sip to calm herself. Her body was in uproar and she knew it. But there was nothing she could do, just watch him as he accepted the drink and moved amongst the revellers: the reception girls and the nurses, Ellie Blake, the secretary, and Katie Gower, practice manager. Everyone had stayed on to make the party a success and Peter was in his element, telling jokes that were horribly old.

Alex smiled, content to try and keep herself in control. To watch him. To let her eyes devour the broad shoulders that her hands had adored and stroked. The long, straight back that her fingertips had caressed. The proud chest that bore the faint scar of the fire and had felt so vulnerable under her fingers.

Long, muscled legs set him a head above the others. She could see the women glancing at him and a little pang of envy beset her, for he was undeniably masculine. Every woman in the room must think so.

But no one else here had felt his skin, she reminded herself lasciviously. No one had touched the smooth, rippled muscle that ran down his abdomen and curved in all the right places. No one but her. And suddenly she was aching so badly to hold him that she could hardly breathe.

For a moment she felt dizzy and drew her eyes down. She looked at her hands, lightly trembling around her glass. Her whole body was in anticipation of his approach and somehow she knew he would be there when she looked up.

'Alex?' His voice flowed over her like a drug.

She raised her face slowly and felt a blow to the stomach that rendered her dumb. She smiled self-consciously and drowned in the grey languid pools that rested on her.

'Aren't you eating?' he asked, jerking one dark eyebrow above the other.

'In a moment,' she said weakly. 'I was enjoying the punch.'

He sat down in the chair beside her and for a moment they were both silent. Her body felt on fire. She couldn't think of what to say—probably because she wanted to say so much, she told herself despairingly.

'Almost there,' he murmured, and she nodded.

'What are you doing for Christmas?'

'I would have taken the call duty, but it was already spoken for.' He glanced at her and she shrugged, trying not to lose her last shred of dignity.

'I thought it was the least I could do,' she answered hesitantly. 'Peter was kind enough to offer me this job, part-time for as long as I wanted, any hours I wanted. Until I really found my feet.'

'And now look at you.' He gazed at her then, his eyes travelling over her face and her soft pale hair and back to her anxious eyes. Was it a flicker of desire that burned in his or was she just fooling herself? 'You look wonderful, Alex.'

Did she look wonderful enough to make him forget everything else and just want to be with her? But then Sean was back again, sinking into the chair beside Daniel, and Alex felt a wave of dismay as Peter strolled over.

As the talking and laughter increased Alex had to be satisfied with Daniel's presence beside her. But she yearned to reach out and touch his strong, broad hand as it fell over the arm of the chair. She recalled what joy it was to touch those fingers and squirm her own around them, feel the heat of his palm, the strength of his grip. In an agony of doubt she remembered every twist and turn they had made in bed, every kiss and sigh that had made that one night so precious.

And here she was, greedy for one glance, a smile, anything that might give her hope. But they might as well be oceans apart. All she could do was torture herself with memories.

She waited, not hearing the noise around them, listening to Daniel's soft laughter, his dark, husky voice as it melted through her bones. Then, somewhere in the room, a phone rang. Alex saw Katie Gower leave her group and go to answer it. Daniel looked up too and Katie beckoned him. He rose and threaded himself towards her, and a few moments later he had the phone locked to his ear.

Alex watched him, heart in her mouth, as he finished the call, shrugged on his coat and left.

In the few days that were left before Christmas Alex resigned herself to acceptance. Daniel didn't want to see her. Maybe, she told herself, it was for the best. What was the point in talking if he'd accepted the job offer abroad? He'd never said otherwise, that he'd stay. She'd known it from the beginning. The sooner she got used to the thought of him going, the sooner she could make her own plans.

What they were, she now had no idea. She'd been so eager to get back to Casualty and hospital life, but now it didn't seem important, or even—and she hated to admit it—appealing. General practice had wormed its way into her soul. And all her other hopes and aspirations seem to fall short.

Would Peter still offer her a partnership? she wondered on the Monday of Christmas week. He might—but then again, was that what she really wanted? Or was it just that she had found something else desirable here?

She couldn't bring herself to imagine what it would be like passing Daniel's empty consulting room or the big house at the end of the road. Perhaps then she'd discover her true feelings and what she wanted to do with her life.

The morning was cold and frosty, a typical winter's morning, and Alex was the first to arrive. She had phoned Cossie's grandparents the night before and they'd assured her Zak was driving Cossie home that evening.

Her spirits lifted, and lifted still more when she read the results of Jane Glynn's fine-needle aspirate cytology. The consultant surgeon, Mr Brace, had written that he'd found no suspicious features in the investigations he'd performed. The lump was benign.

Alex delivered the good news by phone.

'The best Christmas present ever,' Jane said emotionally.

'Come in and see me in six months,' Alex told her. 'Until then, don't forget to self-examine. Once a month, if possible.'

Then she thought—what am I saying? A lot could happen in six months. I might not be here. Oh, Daniel, she thought grimly, what have you done to me? I've no direction any more. I can't think straight.

And it's all because of you.

A little phrase that trickled through her mind until Cossie came home that night. Then, thankfully, he absorbed all her thoughts and she felt almost whole again. Zak was on a high, his marketing deal with a brand-new band signed and sealed.

'Daddy's flying away tomorrow,' Cossie told her that night.

'Yes, I'm sorry, darling. You'll miss him,' Alex whispered as she tucked him into bed.

'Nanna and Pops took me on a big wheel. You can see all over London. But Daddy couldn't come. He had to work.'

'Never mind. Another time, perhaps.'

'I missed you.' Cossie yawned. 'Will Daniel come at Christmas?'

Alex dredged up a smile. She couldn't tell him Daniel was going—not yet. And they probably wouldn't see him over Christmas, but it seemed a sin to say so. Luckily she didn't have to in the end. Cossie's fair lashes dropped and she bent to kiss his blond head.

She left him snoring softly, went downstairs, and wondered for the hundredth time that evening what Daniel was doing.

Alex didn't know how she got through Christmas Eve without phoning Daniel, but she did. She had two calls that night—one a patient who had fallen down the stairs at her daughter's house, the other a teething baby.

Alex suspected a fracture in the adult's arm and admitted her into hospital. But the infant was okay—reacting mainly to its fraught mother. By nine Alex was home. Cossie was in bed and she unearthed the bike and stood it by the tree. Helen transformed it with more tinsel and bows as they listened to the midnight service.

Alex slept fitfully, as she always did when on call, and Christmas Day dawned bright and crisp. Cossie pounced on his bike and Helen and Alex saw to lunch. Jean called, and another of Helen's friends, and half an hour later Ollie and Emma arrived.

'Won't stop,' Ollie said breathlessly. 'We just called to say Happy Christmas.'

'Can Emma come into the garden to see my new bike?' Cossie pleaded.

'All right, but just five minutes, Em. We mustn't be late for Aunty June.'

'How is Emma?' Alex asked as they waited in the hall.

'Much better,' Ollie said brightly. 'I asked Grant to explain to Emma about the new house and she's fine.'

'And you?' Alex asked. 'Christmas must be full of mixed emotions.'

'I've kept myself busy.' Ollie nodded. 'And joined a health club. It's fun; I love it. Did I tell you Grant's partner had a baby son? Born two weeks ago.'

'Oh…' Alex murmured uncertainly.

'I'm okay with it,' Ollie said quickly. 'I've decided this year is going to be a success. I've a new life and I'm determined to enjoy it.'

'Mummy, Daniel's here,' Cossie called from the kitchen, and Alex felt her cheeks flame.

'Oh, well, I won't keep you,' Ollie said, opening the door. 'Cossie, call Emma for me, will you?'

A few minutes later Ollie was driving off and Alex slipped on her coat. She found Daniel and Cossie in the garden and her pulse raced crazily. Daniel was hunkered down, wrapped warmly in a dark jacket and walking boots, and Suzie was wagging her tail furiously as he examined the wheels of the bike.

He stood up when he saw her and grinned. 'I was just wishing I was seven again. It's a great bike.'

She dredged up a smile. 'Thanks. Happy Christmas, Daniel.'

'And to you.' He dug in his pocket. 'Here's something for the tree, Cossie.'

'Can I open it now?'

'If you like.'

Alex shivered as their breath froze in the cold air. A silver glaze covered the trees and speared the ends of the grass. But it wasn't the cold that was affecting her. It was Daniel—the relief of his presence, the joy which suddenly bubbled inside her and made her warm, made Christmas come alive.

He looked so handsome. His dark head was inclined towards Cossie, his luminous grey eyes focused on ten little fingers exploring the gift. His broad shoulders were hunched and she had the insane desire to thread her arms around them.

'Mummy, look!' Cossie exclaimed, holding up a little china seal. 'It looks just like Germaine, the seal from the wildlife park. It is! Look—it's got her name written underneath.'

Alex met Daniel's eyes. 'That's very thoughtful of you.'

'Not at all—and, before I forget, here's a little treat for the spring…'

'Is that for me too?' Cossie asked as Alex opened an envelope.

'For all of you.' Daniel nodded.

'Tokens for Bedlington,' Alex gasped. 'Oh, Daniel, that's wonderful. Will you…' she hesitated '…come in?'

'I'd better get on.' He shrugged, then returned his gaze to Cossie. 'Good luck with the bike, tiger.'

They watched him walk down the garden path to the gate. Suzie followed at his heels, and before he went out he bent to stroke her. Then he lifted his hand and waved. Alex waved back. Cossie jumped on his bike and rode down the path, arriving at the gate as Daniel closed it.

'Thank you for Germaine,' he called, and Daniel grinned and glanced one last time at Alex before disappearing.

CHAPTER THIRTEEN

SHE wouldn't go to Daniel's farewell party. She would lie outrageously to Peter and say that she felt unwell. It was only half a lie, she convinced herself. All that week in January she'd had a cold. It wasn't flu, but it was close, and her legs seemed like rubber contraptions fixed somewhere in between her hips and feet.

If they'd been fairly quiet she would have had a day or two off. But the January rush didn't disappoint. So she turned up in the mornings and trudged home at night, counting the minutes until bed.

'You're pushing yourself too hard,' her mother had warned her.

'I'll take a holiday soon,' she'd promised.

'You'll be too shattered to enjoy it.' Helen had sighed—more than once.

It was better now Cossie was back at school and she didn't have to spread herself so thinly. But under it all was a sense of doom that she couldn't shake.

So she made up her mind to say goodbye to Daniel at work, with the others around if possible. It wouldn't be a formal goodbye. Because she intended to be sick for his party she would just have to make do with a picture in her mind of how he'd last looked. So she came out of the shadows one day and joined them all in the staffroom.

'Not long now, Daniel,' someone said.

'The send-off's tomorrow…'

'The pub, or where?' someone yelled.

'At my place,' someone else volunteered. 'After work. Bring a bottle.'

Alex listened to it all and tried her hardest to smile. And

when she felt she couldn't stand it any more, she summoned her courage and trapped Peter in the office.

'I feel pretty groggy,' she told him. 'I think the worst is over, but—'

'Go home,' he ordered immediately. 'You've looked wretched all week.'

'I'll be in tomorrow…'

'No, you won't. I'll sort out your list.'

'But it's Friday—'

'The last time you had a sick day was half a year ago,' he told her, bundling her coat in her arms. 'Remember? When Daniel first started?'

She remembered with a flash of pain and fought back the tears.

'For once you're being sensible,' Helen said when she arrived home and trailed up the stairs.

Alex collapsed, fully dressed, on her bed. The pictures whirled like shadows behind her closed lids. Daniel beside her, holding her, his grey eyes melting her bones as he made love to her, his fingers trailing over her body like silk. His warmth and tenderness, his passion…and then the ache of loss, swiftly on the heels of desire.

So deep, so cutting.

So final.

And, turning her face into her pillow, she let the tears fall.

She dreaded the phone ringing on Friday, but it didn't. It hurt so much that he didn't ring, and yet it would hurt even more if he did.

On Saturday, the flu—or whatever it was that had brought her low—seemed to lift. Her sea legs returned and she rambled with Cossie and Suzie in the forest, wandering through the gorse and bracken that so gloriously banked the winter woodland.

She closed her mind to the fact that Daniel would be in the air by now. His flight, someone had said, was at two-thirty. She forced herself not to check the time, but when it was dusk she admitted defeat. With the deep red sun at their backs, and a soft grey mist growing in the trees, they headed for home.

On Sunday morning, she asked Cossie what he would like to do.

'Can we ride?' he asked, and though it wasn't the greatest weather she rang the stables. The mist had formed little wet bubbles, dangling from the trees, and Alex was thankful for tough jodhpurs and warm sweaters under jackets.

'Can you find the path?' Rob, the riding tutor, asked. 'It's getting foggy. We don't want to lose you.'

'We'll come back if it's too thick,' Alex assured him.

But it thinned out, her hefty beast knew the path, and Cossie's small grey was content to follow. They'd been out for an hour when the path forked and just ahead of them was Marl Wood and the car park.

Cossie, who had taken the lead, turned in the saddle. 'Can we go that way?' he shouted, and his little horse started.

Alex saw it all in a flash. The abrupt forward movement, the bolt, the loss of stirrups. Cossie's little figure crumbling and tumbling, with a sickening thump, to the forest floor.

She was shaking by the time she'd dismounted and got to Cossie, who lay still, rolled on his side.

His hat had skittered away and his face was white. Please God, let him open his eyes, she prayed, and beat down the nausea.

'Pulse,' she mumbled, talking aloud. 'There… Faint… Oh, Cossie.' Then the professional side of her kicked in and she inhaled slowly, measuring her breath. 'You can't get it wrong now,' she told herself bitingly. 'If you ever do something right, do it now, Alex.'

Mobile phone, she thought, and her fingers fought frantically to find its shape in her pocket. She found it, stabbed numbers—first the ambulance, then Rob. He'd have to take the horses, she thought quickly. The car park was visible through the trees. There was access…they'd get here all right. And again thank God they hadn't been deeper in. Half an hour ago they wouldn't have found them.

'Cossie—I'm here, darling, if you can hear me. I'm here.' She pulled off her jacket and laid it over him, and blessed the horses for staying still. The little grey was nibbling, her reins hanging loose. The big horse was beside her, nosing the undergrowth.

'Hurry up,' she whispered, gently stroking the leaves and bracken from Cossie's quiet pale face.

The nightmare didn't last long. Rob arrived first in his Land Rover. He had a boy with him and in seconds the horses were captured. Rob bent beside her and she tried to tell him calmly what had happened. But when the siren wailed in the distance she almost lost it.

The vehicle slewed to a halt and doors flew open. She tried to be detached, to sound rational and answer all the questions. When the paramedics lifted Cossie into the ambulance all she could do was watch.

'He'll be okay,' Rob said beside her.

'It happened in seconds,' she heard herself bleat. 'There was nothing I could do.'

'Was he wearing his hat?'

She nodded. 'It's over there somewhere.'

Rob went to search, but it was too dark, and by the time he returned she was in the ambulance too.

'Good luck,' he shouted as the doors closed. There wasn't time for more. But the word luck rattled mockingly in her brain. As she looked at Cossie's white face she knew that it was more than luck they would need now.

It was a relief, later, in the intensive care office, to hear Helen's voice on the phone.

'Did the horse bolt?' she asked, sounding stunned.

'No—not exactly. It jumped when Cossie shouted. Then

he lost his stirrups and his hat came off. And…oh, Mum, it all happened so fast.'

'Was he conscious at all?'

'No,' Alex said bleakly.

'I'm coming down, darling—'

'No, Mum. Not yet,' Alex protested. 'There's nothing you can do. We're in ITU and they've done X-rays. When I know more I'll ring you.'

Alex put down the phone. It made no sense for Helen to come in, at least not yet. So she made her way back to Cossie and forced back the tears. She wouldn't weep. Mustn't. If Cossie could hear her…if there was a chance…she had to be strong for him.

Alex sat in the chair at his bedside. The miracle of technology bleeped and winked around him. His eyes were closed, fair half-moons of lashes lying softly on his cheeks. His hair seemed to melt into the pillow and his tiny mouth seemed far too vulnerable for the airway tube.

She held his hand and her lips trembled. The soft little dip of his palm was warm and she whispered that she loved him.

The specialist arrived and they went over the whole thing again. 'Hang in there,' he told Alex, and she nodded, the lump in her throat too big for her to speak.

Then, just when she thought she couldn't do it—she really couldn't just sit by and watch her child die—a hand cupped her shoulder.

'Alex?'

She knew the voice, but it didn't register. And her eyes had been straining so long on Cossie that she could hardly move them upwards. Then suddenly she focused—and thought she must be delusional.

Part of her brain flashed shock. She rose, with shaky legs barely supporting her. Daniel's arms went round her and she buried her face in his shoulder.

'It's all right. I'm here,' he whispered.

'But how…? Why…?' She clung to him, in disbelief and

in wonder, and the tears broke through, flooding down her cheeks and soaking his jacket. He whispered against her ear, soothing her, telling her it was going to be okay, his fingers curving through her hair. She let him comfort her, ashamed to raise her face, ashamed of letting go when she'd tried so hard to be strong.

'Can you go over it one more time?' he murmured. 'For me?'

So she did. Little by little she explained, as he shed his jacket, drew up a seat beside her and listened.

It felt, she thought, a bit like pulling a tooth. But it seemed to help the pain as she told him everything, going through the events that seemed like some terrible dream. Daniel took her hands, and even though she must have repeated herself several times he listened carefully, until finally someone approached.

'Mr Shearing's in the office,' Sister told them quietly. 'He has the X-rays.'

'I'll stay here,' Daniel said, but Alex shook her head.

'I need you with me,' she said croakily.

'Both of you go.' Sister motioned to the door. 'I'll watch here.'

Alex smiled gratefully. She wanted Daniel with her, to help her through whatever she had to face. If it was bad news she didn't trust herself to keep in control.

In the office they listened to what the specialist said. 'Nothing untoward,' he explained carefully. 'At least, not as far as we can see. I'm hoping we'll see an improvement within the next twelve hours.' He paused, and Alex swallowed. 'If not…we'll look at things again.'

She felt sick with fear. What if Cossie didn't wake? What if there was a clot or some obstruction forming? Not everything could be seen on an X-ray. Her mind grappled wildly with the possibilities.

Daniel asked questions that had to be asked whilst she prayed for a miracle to happen to her son.

*   *   *

It was the longest night of Alex's life. They watched, but there wasn't a flicker from Cossie's still little face. They held hands, the three of them, and maintained a vigil, until at last she fell asleep, her head on Daniel's shoulder.

She woke with a guilty start. 'What time is it?' she asked bewilderedly.

'Five-fifteen,' Daniel whispered, running his hand softly down her arm.

'How long was I asleep?' She looked at Cossie but he was just the same, with the tube in his mouth and his eyes closed, his tiny head swamped in the big white pillow.

'Not even an hour.'

'Has anything happened?'

'Not yet.'

She looked at her child again. And love almost broke her heart. How had she let him fall? Had he worn the hat strap properly, under his chin? Could it have snapped in the fall?

They would probably never know.

Then Daniel sat up. 'Alex, I saw something.' He stood and leaned over the bed.

Alex jumped to her feet. 'What?'

'His lashes—they flickered.'

She held her breath and her heart pounded fiercely. 'Yes,' she gasped. 'Cossie—Cossie? Can you hear me? It's Mummy.'

The tiny lids cracked opened. Just a fraction. And Alex couldn't speak for joy as slowly, very slowly, her son came back to her.

Six long, relief-filled hours later, whilst Helen was with Cossie, Alex sat with Daniel in the visitors' room.

She found it inconceivable he was still here, holding her hand, as he done throughout the night. She'd tried to digest all that had happened, but her sleep-deprived brain played tricks on her.

For instance, his last words, she had imagined, were, 'Alex, I love you. I want to be with you always. I hope that you can forgive me for being such a fool.'

Now she stared at him, and he lifted a finger and crooked it against her mouth.

'Just listen, my darling. We've got Cossie back. Safely and without damage. Which makes me want to say so many things. But I'd better say the most important first. I couldn't leave you. I simply couldn't. I'd found you again, only to have you taken away—'

'*Away?*' Alex breathed. 'By whom?'

He didn't answer, but lifted her hand and kissed her fingers. 'When I saw you and Zak together I thought I was too late.'

'But I tried to explain—I tried so hard.'

'I know. And I wouldn't listen. I saw what I wanted to see.'

'But why?' she asked in confusion. 'We'd just… You and I had…'

'We'd just made love, yes. And the shock of seeing you in his arms annihilated me.'

'Oh, Daniel,' Alex sighed, 'Zak's always like that. He doesn't mean anything by it. I know it must have looked as though he did. But going OTT is his way.'

'Yes,' Daniel replied darkly. 'So Peter explained.'

'Peter?'

'At my so-called going away party. In my desperately melancholy state, he sat me down and told me a few home truths. That you weren't in attendance because you'd had to pretend to be ill. And then he asked me what kind of idiot I was, that I'd forced you to tell such a whopper.'

Alex swallowed. 'Peter knew I wasn't ill?'

'Oh, yes. He knew. And he told me it was all my fault. That I'd regret leaving you for the rest of my life. I'd lost you ten years ago, he insisted, and I was about to lose you again.'

'But how did he know about us?' Alex croaked. 'I thought no one did.'

'Well then, you must have been mistaken.'

Alex felt his fingers tighten around hers and she didn't know whether to laugh or cry, so she did a mixture of both—tears and smiles all at once.

His voice roughened then. 'You remember the day I found Stephen in Marl—did you ever wonder why I was there?'

She nodded slowly, recalling Helen's quiet little smile when they'd discussed it later. 'I was in *our* place, thinking of you, of us,' Daniel murmured softly. 'I felt closer to you there than anywhere on earth. And it was quite by chance that I discovered Stephen.'

'Oh, Daniel, I must have been blind. And I'm so ashamed.' She lifted her eyes slowly. 'I gave you an ultimatum all those years ago. I know I must have seemed unreasonably needy, but it wasn't really about your family. It was just that you were away from me and I missed you. I thought I was being sidelined. But you were only doing the best you could for everyone. If only I'd been willing to trust you.'

'Do you trust me now?'

Did she trust him? With all her heart. She trusted him with her life, and Cossie's too, and she knew he would always be there for them. He was the first person Cossie had asked for when he'd come round, and the look of rapture on Cossie's face when he'd seen Daniel had been immeasurable. She had never seen such a look before, not even with Zak. And, though Zak would always be a part of Cossie's life, Alex knew it was Daniel who would be the special one.

So special that it seemed they were purposely designed for each other.

'I trust you, my darling,' she whispered as tears shone like little stars in her eyes. 'I wouldn't have made it through the night without you.'

'Then marry me, Alex. And we'll spend every night together.'

She almost laughed as her breath caught in her throat.

'I mean it, Alex. No half-measures this time. Marry me.'

'But, Daniel—'

'It's all or nothing, Alex,' he told her, his lovely grey eyes intensely serious. 'I'm an old-fashioned guy.'

'But…what about Africa? Your research project? Your commitments overseas?'

'I have only one commitment, Alex. To you and to Cossie. And of course to marrying you as swiftly as is humanly possible, and making you both happy.'

'Do you really want that?' she asked, still uncertain.

'I've done my share for the universe,' he said with a little shudder. 'My life is here. Working with Peter and Sean—and you.'

'Me?' she squeaked. 'But I'm just a locum.'

'I can forgive you for that.' He crooked an eyebrow. 'And there's one more thing.'

'What?'

'I want babies—lots of them. Rosy-cheeked infants that are pure New Forest-bred.'

She giggled. 'If I'm working, how can we do that?'

'Easy.' He shrugged. 'I'll show you.' And, wrapping her in his arms, he kissed her with all the passion of those ten missing years.

'Oh, dear Lord,' she whispered deliriously. 'How much happier could I be?'

'Oh, much more,' Daniel promised huskily. 'Much, much more.'

Modern Romance™
...seduction and
passion guaranteed

Tender Romance™
...love affairs that
last a lifetime

Sensual Romance™
...sassy, sexy and
seductive

Blaze
...sultry days and
steamy nights

Medical Romance™
...medical drama on
the pulse

Historical Romance™
...rich, vivid and
passionate

27 new titles every month.

*With all kinds of Romance for
every kind of mood...*

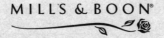

MILLS & BOON®

MB1

MILLS & BOON®

Medical Romance™

ASSIGNMENT: SINGLE FATHER
by Caroline Anderson

Working as a practice nurse in Dr Xavier Giraud's surgery and caring for his children had seemed perfect for Fran after the traumas of A&E. Except she fell in love with him and he could never submit to his love for her in return. Where could her relationship with Xavier go? She was compelled to stay and find out…

MORE THAN A GIFT *by Josie Metcalfe*

After waiting for ever for love, Laurel was devastated when she had to leave consultant Dmitri Rostropovich behind. Now, eight months pregnant and trapped in a snowbound car, she can only wonder if she will ever see him again. Dmitri is searching for her. He's close – very close – but will he find her in time…?

DR BLAKE'S ANGEL *by Marion Lennox*

Dr Blake Sutherland was the sole GP in town – overworked and exhausted, he needed a miracle. He got one in the form of pregnant Dr Nell McKenzie, who insisted she took over his practice! He couldn't possibly let her, so they agreed to share his patients – and Christmas. Blake had a feeling this Christmas would be one he'd never forget…

On sale 6th December 2002

Available at most branches of WH Smith, Tesco, Martins, Borders, Eason, Sainsbury's and all good paperback bookshops.

1102/03a

MILLS & BOON®

Medical Romance™

HOME BY CHRISTMAS by *Jennifer Taylor*

Christmas in the children's intensive care unit is always an emotional time, and especially so this year. Dr Lisa Bennett has until Christmas to decide whether to accept another man's proposal, and consultant surgeon Will Saunders has until Christmas Eve to help her realise that the life she should be daring to share – is his!

EMERGENCY: CHRISTMAS by *Alison Roberts*

Penny only started dating Dr Mark Wallace to make another man jealous – then discovered she'd done the right thing by accident! Their Christmas wedding would be perfect… But now the past was threatening to destroy their love – and a terrifying attack in the emergency room might mean they'd never get a second chance…

CHRISTMAS IN PARIS by *Margaret Barker*

When Dr Alyssa Ferguson returned to work in her beloved Paris, the last person she expected to see was her ex-lover, Pierre Dupont – and now he was her boss! As they began to rekindle their passionate romance, Pierre made Alyssa realise she had to face up to the past. Maybe they could look forward to a blissful Christmas in Paris together…

On sale 6th December 2002

Available at most branches of WH Smith, Tesco, Martins, Borders, Eason, Sainsbury's and all good paperback bookshops.

1102/03b

Double Destiny

There is more than one route to happiness.

Mills & Boon® Tender Romance™ and Medical Romance™ present a gripping, emotional two-part series from leading author **Caroline Anderson**.

Destiny has more than one plan for Fran Williams — it has two: rich, wealthy and energetic Josh Nicholson and charming, sensual, single father Dr Xavier Giraud!

Can a woman choose her own destiny? Could there be more than one Mr Right?

Follow Fran's parallel destinies in:

<u>November 2002</u>
ASSIGNMENT: SINGLE MAN
in Tender Romance™

<u>December 2002</u>
ASSIGNMENT: SINGLE FATHER
in Medical Romance™

Plus *read about Fran's first fateful meetings with Josh Nicholson and Xavier Giraud—for free.*
Look for DOUBLE DESTINY at www.millsandboon.co.uk

1102/02/MB55

MILLS & BOON

CHRISTMAS
SECRETS

Three Festive Romances

CAROLE MORTIMER CATHERINE SPENCER
DIANA HAMILTON

Available from 15th November 2002

*Available at most branches of WH Smith,
Tesco, Martins, Borders, Eason, Sainsbury's
and all good paperback bookshops.*

1202/59/MB50

2 Books
and a surprise gift!

We would like to take this opportunity to thank you for reading this Mills & Boon® book by offering you the chance to take TWO more specially selected titles from the Medical Romance™ series absolutely FREE! We're also making this offer to introduce you to the benefits of the Reader Service™—

- ★ FREE home delivery
- ★ FREE gifts and competitions
- ★ FREE monthly Newsletter
- ★ Books available before they're in the shops
- ★ Exclusive Reader Service discount

Accepting these FREE books and gift places you under no obligation to buy; you may cancel at any time, even after receiving your free shipment. Simply complete your details below and return the entire page to the address below. *You don't even need a stamp!*

YES! Please send me 2 free Medical Romance books and a surprise gift. I understand that unless you hear from me, I will receive 4 superb new titles every month for just £2.55 each, postage and packing free. I am under no obligation to purchase any books and may cancel my subscription at any time. The free books and gift will be mine to keep in any case.

M2ZEB

Ms/Mrs/Miss/Mr ....Initials..........................
BLOCK CAPITALS PLEASE

Surname..

Address..

....

....Postcode ....

Send this whole page to:
UK: The Reader Service, FREEPOST CN81, Croydon, CR9 3WZ
EIRE: The Reader Service, PO Box 4546, Kilcock, County Kildare (stamp required)

Offer not valid to current Reader Service subscribers to this series. We reserve the right to refuse an application and applicants must be aged 18 years or over. Only one application per household. Terms and prices subject to change without notice. Offer expires 28th February 2003. As a result of this application, you may receive offers from Harlequin Mills & Boon and other carefully selected companies. If you would prefer not to share in this opportunity please write to The Data Manager at the address above.

Mills & Boon® is a registered trademark owned by Harlequin Mills & Boon Limited.
Medical Romance™ is being used as a trademark.